LIFE AT THE SHALLOW END

Helen Bailey

*Hodder
Children's
Books*

A division of Hachette Children's Books

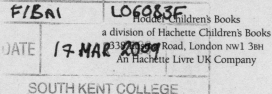

*For Tracey Stratton with love, with thanks,
and without whom this book would be very different!*

Chapter One

What on earth possesses a parent to saddle a child with a ridiculous name like Apple, or Peaches or Dweezil?

Don't these parents have a pang of guilt when they stand in the park shouting, 'Fifi! Come along Fifi!' and a child, rather than a poodle, runs up?

I think there should be some sort of law which allows kids to choose their own name if they don't like the one their parents have lumbered them with. There'd have to be an age restriction of course, like you couldn't pick your new name until you were a teenager, otherwise you might grow up being called Tinky Winky, Barbie or Cinderella, and you wouldn't even have the satisfaction of blaming the parentals as it would be all *your* fault.

'But, darling, *you* wanted that name. We weren't happy, but as it was the law we had no choice but to let you call yourself Snow White. Don't blame us! Blame yourself!'

1

I think it's very important that you suit your name, and how can the parentals know how you're going to turn out when they give you your name at the point in your life when you're nothing more than a screaming wrinkly bundle of skin lying in a cot? Who wants to go to college and have to register as *Angelchild* if there's nothing remotely angelic about you? Or what about if you're called Willow, but look more like a great big gnarled oak tree?

I really understand how minging it is to have a name which doesn't suit your looks or personality, and that's because my parents named me . . . wait for it . . . drum roll . . . Electra. Electra Brown.

Electra! What possessed them? What were they thinking of giving me an exotic Greek name when I'm as English as fish and chips and wet bank holiday weekends, and I've got bog-standard Brown as a surname?

I know what they were *doing*. Mum's older sister, Victoria, and her American husband, Hamp Hampshire, thought they were being all trendy and alternative calling their daughter after the place where she was conceived, a swish apartment on Madison Avenue in New York. So when I was born three months later than my cousin Madison, Mum and Dad thought they'd do the same with me. But I didn't start life in one of New York's smartest streets. I started life in Greece, specifically in the Electra Self Catering Apartments. Mum and Dad haven't actually admitted this of course, they always just say that it's where they spent their honeymoon, but as they had a September wedding and I arrived, late, on the 5th of July, go figure! It could have been worse, I suppose. I could have been named Faliraki Brown.

I am *so* not a Greek girl. Angela Panteli's parents own a restaurant in the High Street, The Galloping Greek, and Ange and her sisters are all olive-skinned, dark-eyed exotic beauties. *Nothing* about me is remotely exotic or Greek. I don't even like moussaka because of the aubergines. Aubergines are vegetables of the devil in my opinion. They taste like a bit of old bath sponge soaked in day-old liquidized vomit and I think there's something deeply suspicious about the sort of people who like vomity veg.

I've got a pale face as wide as a satellite dish, and straight hair that can at best be described as dishwater-blonde, but is really on the light-brown side of mouse. I don't look like I think an Electra should look, I've never felt like an Electra, and I hate it when people say, 'How unusual!' when they hear my name. I don't want to be unusual. If you've got a face like a white dinner plate and mousy hair, you're designed to blend in, not stand out.

And it's hard to blend in when you're called Electra, which if you're not Greek has a slightly dodgy porn-star or drag-queen ring to it.

I don't even suit its meaning. I looked it up once. Apparently it means *The Bright One*.

Hah! Tell *that* to the teachers who take Year 9 at Flora Burke's Community School and they'd have a laugh. Bottom set in French and maths, the only two lessons we're streamed in. Struggling in history and geography. Quite good at English language when I put my mind to it. Ditto Eng lit when I can be bothered to put down *Teen Vogue* and pick up the books we're supposed to be studying. Chemistry? No hope. Biology? Forget it.

I can't even shorten Electra to Ellie because my mum's called Ellie, short for Eleanor, though her family never call her anything other than her full name.

There was a brief phase where I toyed with the nickname Lekky, but then some of the boys at school started saying things like, 'Can I read your meter, Lekky?' with disturbing looks on their already very disturbing zitty-bum-fluff faces, so I abandoned that idea *very* quickly.

I thought about trying an anagram of my name, but the only word I came up with that made any sense was *Treacle*, and names connected with confectionery like

Honey or Candy are truly tragic for anyone over the age of five. Anyway, I'd be in the school register as, *Brown, Treacle*. Enough said.

For my little bro, aka The Little Runt, Mum and Dad decided not to continue with the *Where they did it* theme, and called him Jack, which is a good choice because not only is it ordinary, you can't turn Jack Brown into a daft nickname. There's a boy at school called Frazer Burns, but of course everyone calls him Razor Burns. Everyone except me and my friends who call him Freak Boy behind his back, and FB to his face, *if* we can be bothered to talk to him at all. Freak Boy suits him perfectly as he has this weird nose shaped like a puffin's beak stuck in the middle of his podgy face, and he scuttles around like a beetle, hunched over, reciting ridiculous information such as bus routes and car number plates. A freaky beaky saddo. Even for Freak Boy it could be worse, I suppose. I've heard of someone called Russell Sprout and someone else called Dwain Pipe. Tragic.

Sometimes what starts as a good idea goes horribly wrong.

Take one of my best friends, Sorrel Callender.

Her mum, Yolanda, is a *total* lentil, and has named all her children after herbs. She even runs an organic café called The Bay Tree Café.

The whole herb-name scenario started off well with older sister Jasmine (lovely), then Sorrel (cool and it suits her), but then took an unpleasant turn with Sorrel's younger sister who Yolanda called Senna. Not *Sienna*, which conjures up pictures of sunsets and glamorous film stars, but Senna, known throughout the world as the herb that cures constipation. She's known at junior school as *The Constipation Kid*, and has to put up with jokes about *going through the motions*, and boys coming up to her and asking, 'Keeping regular?' before sniggering and running away. The lack of one little *i* turned the name from film star to laxative. It doesn't help that last time I saw Senna she was an unfortunate-looking child, a large dark-skinned scowly lump with thick specs and braces. I expect she'll just pop in an *i* when she gets older, and her life will become considerably easier, even if she doesn't become prettier.

Even the boys couldn't escape from the herb horror as Sorrel's three-year-old twin half-brothers are named Orris and Basil, but luckily their father, Ray Johnson, Yolanda's partner, seems to have managed to get everyone to call them OJ and BJ.

So, even though unusual names *can* be OK, I still think it's best to choose a regular name.

My other best friend who I've known since primary school is called Lucy. Lucy Malone.

I once asked Luce whether she liked her name and felt like a Lucy, and she looked at me as if I was barking and said she'd never even thought about it. That's why Lucy's such a great name. It fits someone of any age, unlike names like Ethel or Mildred, which could only *ever* be for wrinkly coffin-dodgers.

None of this name-angst applies to pets of course.

We have a guinea pig – though I'd rather have a dog – but I can't believe he sits in his hutch worrying that we've called him Google. Or perhaps he does, which is why he's turned from a cute little bundle of toffee-coloured fur, to a fat demented monster who totally ignores the gorgeous juicy dandelion leaves I offer him and simply launches himself towards me with mad eyes and flaring yellow fangs. I'm looking at this from a guinea pig perspective obviously. I don't *really* think dandelion leaves are tasty, though Sorrel's mum probably puts them in salads. Perhaps as he sinks his teeth into my hand and sees me hop about the garden shrieking, 'I hope the fox eats you!' (I don't really, but those bites hurt and you say things you don't mean in the heat of the moment) he's thinking, *Serves you right for calling me Google, you horrid human.*

The name was Jack's idea as he saw it on the computer and thought it was one of the funniest words he had ever seen. I guess it is when you're young and don't know any better, so proving my point that if you *could* choose your own name, you *must* be made to wait until your age is *at least* in double figures.

Because of the threat of hutch violence none of us dare go near Google now, so Dad feeds him. I say feeds – he approaches the cage wearing an old oven glove and carrying a badminton racket, quickly opens the door, launches a scoop of dried Gourmet Guinea food towards the beast, and beats a hasty retreat. The badminton racket is there just in case Google has quicker reactions than Dad, but so far he's never had to use it to defend himself from unprovoked vicious rodent assault.

Poor Google. He's obviously nuclear angry about *something*. As he got angrier, the less we were able to cuddle him, and so now he just sits, alone, tweeting and twitching, looking at the garden through his cage door, feeling sorry for himself.

I know how he feels. I'm in serious *Why me?* mode at the mo.

And that's not because I've got a dodgy-shaped face, or can't get a date on a Saturday night, or that I've never been allowed a dog, or that I've got the world's most annoying little brother. Those things usually get to me, but today they don't really matter. Not in the grand scheme of life, the universe and everything. That's because yesterday Dad dropped a bombshell into the middle of our quiet ordinary little family.

He's leaving.

Chapter Two

Since Dad announced he was leaving yesterday, I've spent more time than is usual lying on my bed, staring up at the ceiling, trying to make sense of it all. I don't mean just the parentals splitting up, but the usual worries and questions that float constantly in and out of my stressy-head, such as:

Will my face get any wider?

Is my attempt at growing my hair long to try and cancel out the width of my dish-face working, or is it just making me look miserable and my hair seem lank?

Does keeping my fringe make my forehead look smaller with the added bonus of covering up the zits, but is this at the expense of my face looking wider?

When Mum finally lets me dye my dishwater hair, should I go blonde and struggle with dark roots, or dark and risk lighter roots?

How quickly will my roots show up if I go down either the blonde or dark route?

Is it really true that if you shave your legs too young the hairs grow back at twice the usual rate, as if so I've made a lifelong commitment to razors and shaving foam.

If I wear dangly chandelier earrings too often in yet another futile attempt to give the impression of a long rather than wide face, will this accelerate Geriatric Ear Syndrome, i.e. the sort of long thin flappy earlobes with slits for holes you see in wrinkly old coffin-dodgers?

Will I ever get to snog someone for more than just one song?

If, finally, a boy takes an interest in me, how do I know he's not employing the *Befriend the Ugly Friend* tactic, i.e. just being nice to me to get to Lucy who's all blonde and willowy with straight white teeth and perfect skin?

But most worrying of all, will I turn into my mother?

Although I love my mum to bits (except when she nags me about writing thank you letters the *moment* I've opened the present/money-stuffed card/gift voucher) from what I've heard, turning into your mother seems an inevitable consequence of being a daughter.

Mum will sometimes look in the mirror, scowl, run her hands through her straggly hair and say with a sigh, 'God,

I'm starting to look like my mother.' Then she'll turn to me, give me a sort of sad, desperate smile and say, 'They always say like mother like daughter, but until it hits you in the mirror, you never really believe it. It'll be the same for you. We all turn into our mothers eventually.'

This is deeply worrying.

Although I'm tallish like my dad and I've got his wide face, dishwater-coloured hair and pale skin which turns blotchy at the merest hint of a UVA ray, I've got Mum's body shape, which means no waist, a bit of a butt, arms and legs like a couple of unsliced salamis and what our witchy games teacher once called *sturdy thighs*. But what *really* freaks me out is the fear that I may be destined to inherit the curse of the Mighty Mammaries, in other words, Mum's *humungous* boobs. I mean, I want boobs, and a decent-sized pair would be nice, but no right-minded person would look forward to having baps *that* big.

The Mighty Mammaries seem to cover the entire middle-to-upper area of my mother's body. There's no gap between the two body zones. It doesn't help that Mum's quite big all over, not on account of genetics, but because of the amount of chocolate she guzzles, so the overall effect is as if she has one single vast boob stretching from armpit to armpit. A *uni-boob*. If she's not wearing a bra so big a couple of Labrador puppies could sleep in it, then her baps flow down her body and sort of bob about around her waist, so that even the slightest movement left or right can send them swinging out uncontrollably in all directions. It's almost worse if she *does* bundle them into a bap-pack, as then, constrained into one area, they resemble a couple of torpedoes, primed and ready to fire. Boys stop playing football, cars slow down and hoot, and even teachers stare when the Mighty Mammaries make an appearance at the school gates. They're especially noticeable when it's cold as then her nips pop out through her clothes like a couple of champagne corks.

To give you some idea of their size, once, when Lucy and Sorrel were round, Mum bit into a Pringle which shattered, and one half fell down the deep canyon that is her cleavage. She stuck her hand down there (which disappeared!), fished around a bit and then gave up saying, 'Oh, it'll be down there for so long, it'll probably have gone mouldy before I find it again!' The girls were practically wetting themselves with laughter whilst I just wanted to curl up and die of mother-induced shame.

Mum uses her cleavage as extra storage space, tucking in things such as shopping lists, cinema tickets and receipts; a shelf on which to rest boxes of chocolate and cups of tea, and a sort of fleshy battering ram when forcing her way through crowds.

When I lie in the bath and look down at myself – which I try not to do, preferring to camouflage my bod with stacks of bubbles which I strategically arrange over the worst bits – I find it almost impossible to believe that I might have inherited the MM gene. It certainly hasn't made itself known yet. There have been a few bursts of activity around the nipple area, but nothing worth actually wearing a bra for, even though I do, just because everyone does. But I know from doing genetics stuff about fruit flies in science that lurking *somewhere* within my DNA will be the MM gene. The billion-dollar question is, is it recessive or dominant?

It seems pretty dominant to me, especially as Mum's mum, Grandma Stafford, is afflicted, but then on the other hand, from what I remember, Aunty Vicky has the sort of chest that hasn't a hope in hell of catching a falling Pringle.

As cousin Madison turns fourteen in early April, three months before me, I'd *love* to know whether she's sprouted fleshy volcanoes. It's impossible to tell from the photographs Aunty Vicky sends from New York, as every photo we get of the Wunderchild Madison has her holding something in front of her chest, such as a trophy, a certificate or those giant feathery pompoms cheerleaders use. I'm not the slightest bit interested that Madison's been voted girl Most Likely To Succeed in her class, or that she's been appointed class president for the *third* year running. I just want to know her bra size.

With living three thousand miles apart and her being a cheerleader sort and me being, well, not, we're not close. I haven't seen her since I was about ten, when even then she was all cheesy beauty queen material with freakishly shiny chestnut hair and pearly gnashers, so I'd feel awkward emailing her and asking her for her rate of breast tissue growth.

I've thought about making a chart, like a sort of family tree of boobs and the MM gene, to see whether I can work out whether I'm going to be afflicted. To be *truly* accurate I might have to go back a few generations, and the research for that would cause some raised eyebrows. I can just imagine Grandma Stafford's face if I waltzed into her neat little bungalow and said, 'Hiya, Grandma. What bra size do you wear?'

'I beg your pardon, Electra?'

'And how big were your mother's boobs, and those of *her* mother?'

Grandma is *very* prim. The sort of person who says *front bottom* and who refers to the toilet as *the little boy's*

15

room. She even hides the loo roll under a doll with a big pale-pink net skirt.

When Jack was going through his rude phase she looked as if she might faint when he jumped around her living room shouting, 'Farty Poo! Pongy Pee!' so if I mentioned the word *boobs* her head would probably start spinning, her eyes would pop out and then she'd spontaneously combust with shock.

Or perhaps she'd surprise me by saying, 'Ah, now you're old enough to hear the tale of your Great-Great-Great-Grandmother Gertrude, otherwise known as Triple G Gertie, the matriarch of the Mighty Mammary clan, who wore a brassiere as big as a couple of parachutes,' and proceed to tell me all about my big-breasted ancestors, completely missing out their occupations, what they did in the war and who they married, just concentrating on their bra size.

But then again I doubt it.

Knowing my luck I'll be some sort of freaky genetic throwback and have one Mighty Mammary and one minuscule one. A *mono-boob.* As if I haven't got enough to worry about, what with Dad leaving.

Mum doesn't work. She used to work for Dad's plumbing firm, but now I think she just sits around all day, dropping biscuits into the Mighty Mammary canyon and watching Fern Britton – who *definitely* has the MM gene – on telly. Obviously as I'm at school all day I can't *guarantee* that's what she does – she doesn't do it when I'm off with a cold or during the holidays – but during normal life, e.g. during term time, it's a bit suspicious the number of times she will say, 'Fern said this' or 'Fern did that' as she's pottering about the kitchen. Mum only *ever* potters. Moving fast is something alien to her, probably on account of the weight of those vast baps she has to lug about.

I've made Mum-sized boobs out of mounds of bubble-bath bubbles to try them out for size, but every time I do, I panic and slip under the water to get rid of them, their size is so terrifying. I *so* hope that I grow ordinary normal ones.

I'm doubly-doomed on my chances of inheriting enormous baps, as even my dad has boobs. *Man-boobs!* Mostly his moobs are hidden by his extra-large polo shirts, but they're revealed in their true pale and wobbly hideousness as soon as the sun shines and he strips off. I'd say he's *easily* a 44B.

As well as the *like mother like daughter* thing, there's also *like father like son*, so by the time he gets to my age I expect Jack will start to worry that he's going to grow boobs too.

Dad works. All the time. Even weekends and evenings. He never seems to stop and nor does his moby. Sometimes we'll just be sitting down to eat, his phone will ring and he'll answer it, and Mum doesn't even need to be told he's going out, she's already putting his plate back in the oven.

He runs his own company, Plunge It Plumbing Services. Mum encouraged Dad to start the business once they were married, and whilst he dealt with pipes and poo Mum did the books, sorted out the invoicing, the VAT and that type of thing and did a business secretarial course in the evening. When they first started they couldn't afford a proper van, so Dad bought an old ice-cream van, took the giant cone off the top, replaced it with a huge plastic plunger and went around in that. He loves to tell the story of how at first he kept the tune and would set it off just as he approached the house where the plumbing crisis was happening. He had to stop as kids came rushing into the street when they heard the tinkly chimes of Bobby Shaftoe playing, but then bawled their heads off when they found a man holding a length of copper pipe, rather than an ice cream with a Flake stuck in the top.

In the last few years the business has really grown and now Dad employs loads of staff. He owns a large officecum-warehouse on an industrial estate on the outskirts of town, and has a fleet of blue and white Transit vans ready to deal with every kind of plumbing emergency.

There's a domestic team which deals with ordinary plumbing problems such as nappies stuffed down U-bends and blockages of nasty stinky waste (don't even think about it!) and a new division Dad started about eighteen months ago, which handles big commercial contracts, such as plumbing hundreds of toilets into a new sports stadium.

I don't understand it. They managed to stick together through the ice-cream-van years when money was tight, so why not now?

I haul myself off my bed and go down a flight of stairs to Mum and Dad's room and put my head around the door. The big double bed hasn't been made and there are Mum's clothes all over the floor and books piled up on her bedside table. Dad's bedside table is empty except for the radio alarm.

I go over to Mum's dressing table and pick up the framed photograph of the parentals on their wedding day, over fourteen years ago. It's odd to think I didn't exist when the photo was taken. In it, Mum and Dad look really happy, though I'm amazed Mum wasn't mortified by the size of the white satin meringue she'd chosen to wear and the massive bunch of white lilies she's clutching. You can just see Dad's mum, Nana Pat, holding a cigarette down by her side. Granddad looks proud of Mum and is beaming, but Grandma has a face like thunder under her massive lilac hat. She still looks like that when Dad is mentioned. She's never forgiven him for enticing her daughter away from her studies to walk down the aisle.

Eleanor Charlotte Stafford met Robert 'Rob' Brown on the beach on holiday in Fuengirola in Spain. Mum had just finished her GCSEs and Dad had completed his plumbing course at the Tec. It's just *so* typical of my mum to go all the way to Spain, ignore all the bronzed Spanish lurve gods and cop off with a lobster-red English guy with moobs. Grandma was apparently *nuclear* furious that although Mum did A levels she refused to go to university because she didn't want to leave Dad and wanted to get married as soon as she was eighteen, and there were some *mega* rows over her getting hitched so young.

I put down the photo.

I bet you right now Grandma is wagging her finger at Granddad and crowing, 'I told you holiday romances never last.'

Chapter Three

I haven't been able to think straight since the Big Announcement. It's been just over twenty-four hours since they told me and my brain is all over the place. One minute I'm thinking *Dad has left us!* whilst lying on my bed with my iPod plugs rammed in to my ears, listening to 'American Idiot' at eardrum-bleeding levels, feeling sorry for myself, and the next I'm wondering *Does green eyeliner complement or clash with blue eyes?*

I can be *very* shallow.

I find it hard to concentrate at the best of times. Mrs Frost, aka The Penguin, my form teacher and Head of English, wrote in my last school report, *Electra has a brain like a butterfly, both in terms of its ability to concentrate on one subject for more than a millisecond and also, possibly, its size.*

Spiteful mare.

All I can say is at least no one will ever nickname *me* The Penguin.

Mrs Frost has an odd waddling walk because she has no ankles. I expect that anatomically she has ankles or she wouldn't be able to stand up – unless she's being held up just by two columns of fat and water – but because her legs are so porky, the flesh sort of flows down her legs, over where her ankles should be, across the top of her feet and down the sides of her sandals. She *always* wears tights and sandals, summer *and* winter. I don't think that amount of flesh can be forced into proper shoes. The sandal and tights combo just about constrains her feet, but I imagine that without them her feet would spill over the floor like big fatty splats. Her trotters are probably webbed too. With wearing sandals all the time you can see her toes are just one big blob. I feel sick even thinking about them.

Frosty's waddling walk, the fact that her arms seem *way* too short for her body, and because she wears a black skirt, black cardigan and white shirt, *every day*, means she looks exactly like a penguin, except not so cute. Not cute at all. On the other hand, Frosty the Penguin has a husband who apparently has been with her for thirty-five years. *Thirty-five years!* How come my dad leaves my mum after fourteen years, yet a woman with no ankles, webbed feet and the dress sense of a smelly fish guzzler can keep her husband for more than twice the time?

Anyway, where was I? Yes, remembering what happened yesterday. The Big Announcement.

I'd spent the morning at Lucy's hoping that I'd see the love of my life, the man I am destined to be with *for ever*, even though he's not aware of it yet, The Spanish Lurve God, Javier Antonio Garcia, or Jags, as he is known. He has the most fantastic dark eyes, black hair gelled into a peak at the front, long spidery eyelashes and just a hint of proper stubble, unlike the Zitty Bum Fluff Burke's boys in my year. Lucy admits Jags is good-looking even if she thinks he plasters his hair with too much greasy gel, but Sorrel is snippy about him saying he looks *short and agricultural*. I'm not sure what she means by the agricultural jibe, but she always says it with a sneery curled lip so it's obviously not intended as a compliment. Personally I find the thought of Jags sitting astride a tractor or milking a cow rather thrilling.

Lucy says Jags wasn't born in Spain *or* on a farm, he comes from Slough, although his dad is originally from Seville. I know about the Seville connection because once I found out Jags' dad is a doctor at the local hospital I did extensive Internet stalking and found a write-up on a medical website. Dr Antonio Garcia is apparently an

23

orthopaedic surgeon, a leading specialist in replacing hip and knee joints, and enjoys golf when he's not sawing through bones. Lucy knew of the link with Slough as Jags is friends with Lucy's older brother James. They're both in Year 10 at King William's School for Boys, a positive oasis of tasty testosterone compared to Burke's, which is a total desert, devoid of *any* talent. Having an older brother is so much more useful than having a younger one, especially a brother that goes to a different school, *and* an all-boys' school at that. Lucy's got a much older brother, Michael, but he's a useless source of fresh meat as he's in his first year at Imperial College London, and according to Luce, studying the art of having a good time and getting drunk in between a Chemical Engineering degree.

Anyway, neither James nor Jags was at Lucy's house, and as she had no idea where James had gone and, rather meanly I thought, refused to phone him to find out, I couldn't stalk James in the hope of a Jags-sighting. Instead, we spent the early afternoon having a glorious gossipy bitch-fest about a party we'd been to just before Christmas, and perfecting the research project of my life, the Snogability Scale.

The Snogability Scale has five levels and is based purely on looks, not on actual snogging competence. It could only be based on looks, as although I've spent *years* practising on my arm, my actual snogging experience is limited to being grabbed and snogged by a French exchange student called Didier during the last song at a school disco last summer. I don't know what *last resort* is in French, but I'm sure that's what I was. I wasn't even worthy of a snogfest, just a one-song snog without proper tongues before he got on the coach to get the ferry home. It was *horrible*. You'd think a French boy might know how to French kiss, but Didier Deville really let his country, and me, down. It was like being snogged by one of those machines at the dentist, all noise and suction, making your mouth dry whilst showering the rest of your face with spit and water. It's one of the few times I've been grateful for being dire at French, otherwise I'm sure that when the Froggy boys were leaping around and gabbling as the lights went up and the DJ started packing up his kit, I'd have understood what they were saying, which was almost certainly, 'Didier copped off with a satellite dish!'

Quite frankly, I'm feeling the pressure to get at least a *bit* more experience under my low-slung belt. It's not so bad for Luce as she has plenty of opportunity, even though she does nothing about it. Boys *love* her. Sorrel just doesn't seem to bother with boys unless she's telling them to get lost, so she doesn't care. I *do* care, but I've never had the opportunity.

I don't understand it.

All the mags tell you that teen boys are horny creatures, ready to feel up your shirt or down your knickers at the merest hint of an invitation. Forget the coy looks and come-hither eyes. I could send out actual printed invitations – *Electra Brown invites you to 14 Mortimer Road to view the latest stage in the development of her bust* – and I don't think anyone would turn up.

It doesn't stop me working on perfecting the S-Scale though.

1S – Not snogging but mouth-to-mouth resuscitation. You'd need to be either comatose, anaesthetized or preferably dead before the smackers of a 1S boy would ever get near you. Quite frankly, the only way I could *ever* see me getting anywhere *near* a 1S boy is if I needed the kiss of life for serious medical reasons, such as impending death. But then I'd need hypnotherapy afterwards to erase the memory. I'm keen to expand my kissing repertoire beyond the sucking Frog, but I'm not *that* desperate.

2S – You could allow one single short snog, definitely no tongue and tonsil action, as long as no one was watching, and only if it was to prevent some major life-threatening action with far-reaching consequences for the world, such as the end of civilization or to avert some major terrorist attack. In other words, you would be snogging for mankind, *not* for your own enjoyment.

3S – A sort of take-it-or-leave-it type of snog score, suitable for the average-looking boy. Didier the Snogging Frog was a 3S in theory, but below the scale in practice. For a 3S it's OK if you're seen together, OK if you aren't. A sort of *could do better* choice of snogging partner.

4S – Now we're getting into the serious stuff. The jump from 3S to 4S is quite considerable. Championship to Premier League. A 4S boy is almost certainly cool and sporty, at *least* a year above you and probably at a different school. 4S on the scale is a boy that you *definitely* wouldn't want to snog in private, well, not *just* in private, as it would be imperative that *all* your friends saw you, knew that you were snogging a 4S specimen and so were made to feel *hideously* jealous.

5S – The pinnacle of the scale. You can go no further. Completely unobtainable, except in your dreams. Cool, sporty, looks to die for and every girl in every local school after him. You would probably only remember the first nanosecond of a snog with a 5S boy having fainted dead away at the first touch of his lips, collapsing in an unattractive drooling heap at his feet. The Spanish Lurve

God Jags fits in to this category.

There are of course scores in between the different levels, e.g. it is rare for someone to be an outright 3, more likely a 2.9 or a 3.1, and Luce and I had only got to discussing who at the Christmas party might be a 3.4 when Mum rang me on my moby.

'Electra, love, can you come home?' Her voice was wobbly, but I thought she'd just overdone the Christmas chocolate and was having a blood sugar crash.

'Now?'

'Yes *now!*'

I was about to ask why and plead my case for staying longer when the phone went dead, so I left Lucy's and got on the bus to go home, furious and *determined* to be as sullen as possible in retribution for being summoned back without a valid explanation.

When I saw Dad's van parked in Mortimer Road I thought it was odd that he was home at four o'clock in the afternoon on January 2nd. The holidays for non-school people were officially over, which usually means there's some plumbing disaster like a leaking toilet and sewage all over the boardroom which has only just been discovered once the offices have reopened after the break.

Even though he could afford a nice car, Dad still drives

one of the fleet vans. He says he's still a *down and dirty* plumber at heart, and driving a van fully loaded with tools makes him feel part of the team, plus it's like a moving advert, what with the website and phone number plastered down the side. If he needs a proper car he uses Mum's old silver Golf.

I went in to the house, chucked my coat over the end of the banister, arranged my face into its most sullen mode, and clattered downstairs to our basement kitchen.

Mum was sitting at the kitchen table and Dad was standing, leaning against the dresser. Jack had jumped on to the table and was perched on one corner, swinging his legs. I hovered by the table to make it quite clear that I didn't want to be there, had only returned home under sufferance, and was on my way back out or up to my room as soon as possible.

'So?' I asked accusingly, the combination of a sullen face and monosyllabic questions (and answers) being particularly effective in letting otherwise emotionally ignorant parents know that you are *not* happy.

'We've got something to tell you,' Dad said. 'Something important. A big announcement.'

I thought he looked a bit sweaty and uncomfortable, but decided that might be because, for once, he didn't have his mobile phone clamped in his hand.

'You're going to take me to Arsenal!' Jack shouted, and started swinging his legs faster. 'Cool!'

Dad looked even more uncomfortable. I don't know how Mum looked – I wish I'd noticed – but I was too busy trying to stop Jack from kicking me with his wildly swinging legs, whilst keeping my *Am I bovvered?* look intact.

'Er . . . well, I will, but that's not it.' Dad was shifting from one leg to another. Jack was still swinging his legs. I was getting dizzy with so many lower limbs in motion around me.

'Well?' I asked, glaring at no one in particular and then rolling my eyes for added impact.

'This isn't easy,' Dad said. 'It's never a good time for this type of thing. It will be a change for you, for all of us, but . . .'

Mum gave a sort of watery snort and *then* I looked across at her. She looked pale and unwell. *Peaky* as Nana Pat would say. She hadn't been herself since just before Christmas, and even for Mum she was moving about slowly, not so much tortoise-slow as nearly-dead-slug-slow. I'd heard her being sick a few times over the holidays, but when I asked her what was wrong she just said she was under the weather and I didn't think anything of it. But now I realized. I put it all together. The sickness, Mum looking pale and being so tired; the whispering (which I thought was about my Christmas pressie which turned out to be a digi camera, slim, silver, completely gorgeous, millions of pixels). There was only one conclusion.

'Oh. My. God. You're preggers! You're going to have another baby!'

There was no *way* I could keep up the sullen face and monosyllabic combo faced with this *horrific* news.

I thought Dad was going to slide down the side of the dresser and under the table he looked so shocked. He pulled out a chair and sat opposite Mum at the table.

Jack shouted, 'Gross,' and then asked, 'Can I teach it to be a goalie?'

'No!' Mum gasped in a squeaky voice. 'That's not it!'

She looked even paler.

Then my heart started fluttering and my stomach churned as my butterfly brain began to search for possible other reasons for the Big Announcement.

Naturally it alighted on a terminal illness.

'You've got cancer!' I screamed, jumping up and down. 'Are you going to die?'

Jack had stopped kicking the chair and was looking scared. I'm sure I was looking scared. I know I felt it.

'No! No!' Mum cried.

'We're not handling this very well,' said Dad. He was slumped over the table on his elbows, grinding both wrists into his eye sockets.

'You mean *you're* not handling it,' Mum snapped, glaring at him.

She looked across at Jack and me and I noticed she was shredding a tissue in her hands, dropping the bits on to the table and brushing them on to the floor.

'What your dad is *trying* to tell you is that he's . . . we've . . . decided to separate.'

'Split up,' Dad explained to Jack who was still looking scared and now confused. 'I'm moving out this afternoon. I'm going to stay with Nana Pat for a bit, just until we decide what's going to happen next.'

I'd like to tell you *loads* about how I felt at that moment, you know, a blow-by-blow account of the seconds after Dad dropped the *I'm leaving* bomb into the middle of our family, but I honestly can't. I'm not fudging it or putting it to the back of my mind or burying it so I don't have to face up to it. I am *so not* in denial. I felt nothing. It was as if my mind went blank for a bit. Numb. Sort of like what happens when Mademoiselle Armstrong suddenly picks on me to answer a question in French oral, but a *hundred* times worse. Perhaps it's like having a blow on the head? You feel a sudden terrible wave of dizziness crash over you, your eyes go all swimmy and then *nothing* until you come to and people are crowded around, staring down at you, and you hear the siren of an ambulance hurtling towards you. I've never been hit on the head, well not an Accident & Emergency-visiting-serious-blow-on-the-head-type hit, but I've seen how they do it on the telly. It was a bit like that, but without the sirens.

The next thing I remember thinking was *I know I failed the entrance exam for Queen Beatrice College for Girls –* poor non-verbal reasoning apparently – *but how could I have been so stupid as to one minute honestly believe that the parentals were going to have a baby, when the next they're telling us they're splitting up?*

I became aware of everyone talking around me.

'Who's going to play table football with me?' Jack was demanding.

Dad said, 'Well, I will. It's not like I'm not going to be popping round.'

Popping round! I thought. *Popping round! How come it's got to the point where Dad is talking about popping round and I didn't even notice?*

'But I might not *want* to play when you're here,' Jack cried. 'And what if I *want* to play when you're not?'

'I'll play with you.' Mum had tears in her eyes and no tissue left to shred.

Jack jumped off the kitchen table and screamed, 'I don't want to play table football with you. I want to play with Dad. *You're* bloody crap!' and stormed out of the room.

I expected Mum or Dad or both to follow him, telling him off for swearing, but they didn't, which is mega annoying as The Little Runt will think he can get away with swearing all the time now.

'Electra?' Mum's voice was squeaky. 'You've been very quiet. You haven't said anything.'

'Is there anything you want to ask?' said Dad. His voice was wobbly. 'Anything you want to say to us?'

I began to scream at both of them.

'You know this is going to ruin my life, don't you? You know I'm going to have to have *years* of therapy to get over this? I'm now just a statistic from another broken home! If I turn to drink or drugs or go out with boys who have ASBOs and get pregnant, then it'll be *all your fault*. If I fail my GCSEs and end up begging outside Sainsbury's for the pound coin from the trolleys, then you'll only have *yourselves* to blame. Couldn't you have waited until I was old enough not to care, like when I'm thirty or something! How *could* you be so selfish?'

Actually I didn't say any of those things. I wanted to, but my brain and my mouth didn't seem to be communicating, and my throat felt as if someone had rammed a nail file down it and was filing away at my tonsils. So all I said to Dad was, 'If you're leaving, who's going to feed Google?'

Chapter Four

'So who *is* feeding the psycho pet?' asks Sorrel, when I tell her and Luce Dad has moved out.

I tell them sitting in Burger King. I usually tell Lucy and Sorrel *everything* the *moment* it happens, but this time I waited a couple of days before I spilt the break-up beans. Having gone through the kitchen scene in my mind about a zillion times, I was just too tired to go through everything again, and I also thought that in a few days I might make sense of the situation. To be honest, I also felt sure that Dad would come straight back from his mum's, realizing that whatever it was he didn't like about living at home, it wasn't as bad as living with Nana Pat, who is great to visit but would drive you nuts on a full-time live-in basis, what with her chain-smoking, constant burping and telly blasting at full volume all evening. Nana Pat lives on her own as Dad's dad, Kevin, died in an

36

accident on a building site just after I was born. He fell in to a deep pit of wet concrete and drowned. It was tragic at the time, and now I'm older I can see that, but when I was young his death was a constant source of fascination to me and I was always asking Nana Pat questions about the accident. Did he set in the concrete? Did he have to be chipped out? Did he look like a stone statue? Was his coffin extra heavy because of the concrete? As he was cremated, can concrete burn? Poor Nana. It must have been dreadful for her, but she took all my questions in good spirits and never seemed to mind.

Anyway, Mum seems pretty calm about the whole thing, just pottering about as usual, though I would say she has upped her chocolate intake quite dramatically. Dad's been back several times during the last couple of days just to pick up odd bits of post, change a light bulb and feed Google. Things seem so normal, I did begin to wonder whether I'd had some sort of weird vivid dream, and the whole Big Announcement scene was a figment of my overactive imagination. I felt I needed proof that I wasn't hallucinating, so when Mum was in the kitchen I went into their bedroom and looked in Dad's wardrobe. There was mostly wire hangers, dust balls and no clothes or shoes, so he must have gone.

We're in Burger King because Sorrel has spent

the entire Christmas break without meat, and has become desperate to feel some cooked flesh between her gnashers. So whilst Lucy and I are sitting with a chocolate milkshake (me) and a Diet Coke (Luce), Sorrel is ripping into a flame-grilled extra-large bacon double cheeseburger.

All the Herbs, even Parsley their cat, have been brought up vegetarian, which sends Sorrel *mental*. Her mum has declared their house a *Face Food Free Zone*, in other words, anything that has had a face but is now dead can't come anywhere near the house to be eaten. Yolanda made a sign for the front door, but as cats can't read Parsley ignores the instruction, and regularly drags half-dead birds with flapping wings and fully dead mice with blood oozing out of tooth-inflicted puncture wounds into the house before eating them. This makes Yolanda scream at the cat and Sorrel shout at her mum, 'It's nature!' whilst feeling jealous that Parsley is devouring a good meaty meal when she has to eat nut rissoles and brown rice which looks like maggots. Sorrel claims that sometimes she gets so desperate for proper food she just hangs around the door of Burger King, sniffing the meat juices in the air. She's not worried that her mum will see her – Yolanda would *never* shop anywhere *near* a burger bar – but as she shares a bedroom with Jasmine she does worry about her sister smelling meat on her breath and telling her mum, which means the money Sorrel doesn't spend on burgers, she spends on mouthwash. Poor Sorrel. Other kids worry about whether their parents will find out they smoke. Sorrel worries that her mother will find out she's eaten a piece of cow sandwiched between two pieces of white bread.

The vegetarian thing almost got out of hand when Yolanda flirted with veganism, but Sorrel threatened to leave home and put herself into care if she wasn't allowed cheese, milk or eggs. No wonder her mum and her argue all the time. Whatever Yolanda says or does, Sorrel says or does the opposite, just to wind her up. She might be a bezzie, but I'm not blind to the fact that she can be a right cow when she wants to be.

Back to the guinea pig.

'Dad feeds him,' I say. 'He's been coming over every night after work.'

'So he'll come back for the mental mammal, but not for your mum?' Sorrel raises an eyebrow. 'That's *well* weird.'

I hadn't thought of it that way.

Lucy squeezes my arm. 'What a shock! You must be totally wiped out by it all. I can't imagine my mum and dad *ever* splitting up.'

That's what I would have said only a few days ago, and

look at me now! A statistic! All the same, I would have to agree with Lucy that the thought of her mum and dad separating is totally off the radar. Bella and Tom Malone are like grown-up versions of the coolest, most popular kids at school.

Lucy's dad owns Home Malone, a chain of estate agents. He looks immaculate, has clean fingernails, shiny blond hair, wears coordinating ties and shirts, drives a big silver Mercedes and always has his hands-free moby kit stuffed in his ear.

Bella calls herself a *Home Stylist* which seems to involve a lot of driving about the country and trips to France to buy cheap fancy mirrors, old chairs and odd lamps, which she then tarts up and sells to big department stores for quadruple the price.

Everything about them is neat and shiny and coordinating and perfect.

Bella never chips a nail or gets spots. Her teeth glow white and her bobbed hair is always the same mixture of honey-blonde and buttery-yellow streaks. She *never* has roots. She can drive in high heels. Her purse matches her handbag. Lucy *says* her mum uses fake tan, but I've never seen Bella with telltale streaky orange legs. Beneath her pristine white shirts lurks a pert chest. There are never any sweet wrappers in her car, which I think is unnatural. I expect she even farts perfume.

Bella is a total Neat Freak which makes me nervous when I'm round at Lucy's. Their house is so neat and tidy it's like something out of a glossy mag. I'm always *terrified* I'm going to tramp muddy footprints on to their designer rugs or spill Coke on the sofa which is covered in creamy linen and looks hideously expensive and too perfect to sit on.

The Neat Freak has banned Lucy from doing normal messy things like leaving shoes in the hall or mugs in her bedroom. Luce can't even put posters on her bedroom wall with Blu-Tack. She has to give them to Bella, who frames them and hangs them using picture hooks and a spirit level, but only if they go with the colour scheme of Lucy's room which is all beige and cream and coordinating, and a bit too grown up, it being chosen by a Home Stylist. Lucy thought she could get around the picture ban by sticking things on the *inside* of her wardrobe door, but there's no escape from the manicured clutches of The Neat Police, and Bella ripped them all off when she found them, telling Lucy how disappointed she was in her lack of style and making her arrange her CDs in alphabetical order as punishment.

I wonder what The Neat Freak would make of my room? The walls are painted in Dulux *Babe* pink and *covered* in pics and bits, and the laminate floor is littered with *stuff*. Even my mum, who's so untidy sometimes I call her Queen of the Grubs, says it's like a sty in the sky, given that it used to be the loft before it was converted. I've obviously inherited mum's Chaos and Clutter gene, though unlike the Mighty Mammary gene, the C&C DNA made itself known when I was still in nappies.

No, there's *no way* that Bella and Tom would ever do anything as messy as split up.

'I bet he's got a bit on the side,' says Sorrel, munching away.

'As if!' I shock myself by almost shouting above the piped music. 'He'd have told us, or Mum would tell me.'

In one of my many lying-on-my-bed-staring-into-space sessions, I *had* considered the possibility of Dad having some hot totty squirrelled away, perhaps one of the girls in the office, or some desperate housewife who needed plumbing advice and was impressed by the size of Dad's extensive tool box, but concluded that he was much too busy organizing the unblocking of toilets to have the time. He certainly doesn't have the looks. It isn't just that he's going bald and has a bit of a pot belly and moobs, he dances *really* oddly. He sort of clenches his fists and does strange jerky movements with his upper body whilst his feet remain in one spot as if he's having some sort of seizure. No one could possibly fancy a man who dances like that, could they? I mean, I know Mum did, once, but as Grandma always says, she was young and didn't know any better. Is Dad fanciable to someone? I always think of fanciability and snogability as one and the same, but to even *think* about the S-Scale in relation to your dad is sick, even if you are applying the scale on behalf of someone else, so I have no idea whether Dad is fanciable or not. He's just, well, Dad.

'So, when are they getting divorced?' Sorrel asks with her mouth full.

'They're not! It's just a trial separation.'

I say this in what I hope is a convincing voice, even though it's not actually true. No one had mentioned the word *trial* but Dad had said that he was going to stay with Nana Pat and I can't see him staying there for long. What he'd actually said was 'until we decide what's going to happen next,' and the tension of not knowing what's going to happen next is playing havoc with my skin.

'When did they tell you?' asks Lucy.

'Monday afternoon. No, Tuesday! Monday! What day is it today? God, my head's trashed.' I seem to have lost all track of the days since the Big Announcement and I'm struggling to think. 'It must have been Monday. The day after New Year's Day. When I got back from coming round to yours.'

'I *knew* something was up,' says Lucy. 'Your mum rang my mum in the morning. There was loads of whispering in the hall and then Mum came through and asked me to ask you to come round.'

'You didn't text *me* to come over,' Sorrel mutters.

'Sorry.' Lucy looks guilty. 'You said you were stuck with looking after the twins so I didn't think you'd be able to.'

'So when you texted me, it was just because your mum had told you to?' I feel annoyed that the parentals are secretly organizing my social life behind my back.

'Well, I was going to anyway,' she says. 'Mum just beat me to it.'

'What else did she say?'

Lucy shrugs her narrow bony shoulders. 'Nothing, at the time. But then, when you'd gone, I heard her on the phone to Dad and she said something like, "Rob's told Ellie."'

'And you didn't you think to tell me?' I grumble. 'Couldn't you have warned me what was about to happen? Were your texting fingers frozen?'

I start picking at a spot on my chin that I squeezed yesterday, even though I know it's the number-one skin sin, but when your parents are separating you need *some*

44

fun, and for the brief moment I heard the little *phut* noise and the creamy pus hit the mirror at supersonic speeds I felt relieved and happy.

'I never thought,' replies Lucy. 'I didn't make the jump from what I heard Mum say to the fact that your mum and dad are getting divorced.'

'Sep-ar-ra-ted,' I correct her firmly, as a huge lump of scabby skin covered in Rimmel Hide the Blemish in *Fair* drops on to the table. I look at my finger. I've made the spot bleed so I press a white shiny serviette on it, hoping to stem the flow of blood. 'No one's said *anything* about divorce.'

Sorrel is busy licking her fingers, determined not to waste even a trace of precious meat juice. 'He hasn't just upped and gone for no reason, you know. I *bet* he's been unfaithful. Men always are.' She looks longingly over my shoulder at the menu above the counter. Christmas holiday meatless-meals with the family means she has some serious catching up to do on the flesh front. 'That's why my mum and dad split up, remember. Dad succumbed to sins of the flesh.'

This is true, but not in the way it sounds.

Sorrel's mum caught Sorrel's dad greasy-handed, eating a bacon sarnie in the back garden when he thought Yolanda was out at the café all day. There was a terrible row

45

and he confessed to eating meat behind Yolanda's back for *years*. Yolanda went nuclear mental and said, 'It's us or Face Food,' and Desmond Callender chose Face Food and fled back to his native Barbados where he's set himself up as an artist with a studio in the capital, Bridgetown.

Sorrel has us in hysterics when she does an impression of her dad saying in a strong West Indian accent, 'But, woman! A man can't live a decent life without fried flying fish or meat pepper pot!! It's unnatural, I tell you!'

'It's not the same thing at all,' I say to Sorrel.

'It is,' she says, getting all stroppy. 'It's still breaking a vow.'

'I didn't think your mum and dad were legally married,' says Luce.

Sorrel rolls her eyes. 'Duh! I meant the vow of vegetarianism he took when he met Mum. By eating meat he gave in to temptation and broke that vow.'

'Er, the words *pot*, *kettle* and *black* come to mind, Miss Flesh Ripper,' I say laughing, checking the serviette to see whether the zit has stopped seeping blood, which thankfully it has.

Sorrel looks irritated. 'I never made a promise I knew I couldn't keep. Dad did. When he promised to be faithful to the cause, forsaking all meat until death did them part, he knew he could never keep to it. He knew he'd keep a bit of bacon on the side.' She glares at us, tosses her beaded braids, and pushing her chair back stomps off to order something else.

'How's your mum?' asks Lucy.

'Seems normal. Eating lots of chocs. Watching lots of telly.'

'What's she said?'

'About what?'

'About why your dad left!' Lucy sounds a bit exasperated at the lack of info.

I expect that if the unthinkable happened and Bella and Tom *did* split up, they'd sit Lucy, James and Michael down and have a very grown-up conversation, discussing all the facts. Bella would probably make a spreadsheet, all in tasteful colours of course, a timetable of what was happening and when it was going to happen which she'd laminate and hand round.

Or maybe she'd make a PowerPoint presentation:

Slide One The Malone Family. This is Your Divorce.

Slide Two How Did it Happen?

Slide Three What Happens Next?

And so on. Sorrel comes back with a Chicken Whopper. 'What have I missed?' she asks.

'I've just been asking Electra what her mum has said about her dad leaving,' replies Lucy.

'And?' Sorrel says.

'Nothing,' I reply.

'Haven't you pumped her for info?'

I shake my head.

'And little Jack. Has he said anything?'

More head-shaking.

'Not even to you?'

'Nope.'

'Girlfriend!' exclaims Sorrel, the chicken rolling around her mouth like clothes in a tumble dryer. 'You lot are un-bloody-believable! Your old man announces he's leaving. You've said nothing, bro's kept quiet, and your mum can't speak for filling her gob with chocs. Talk about a family of clams!'

Sorrel's right. When it comes to discussing problems we *are* as tight as clams. The Browns operate on the principle that if you don't talk about it, it either doesn't exist or it will go away. We've *never* been the sort of family to sit down and discuss things.

Take Sex Education.

For Lucy's thirteenth birthday Bella created a 'Sexucation Question and Answer' pack complete with hand-drawn diagrams for Lucy and her to go through, *together*. Luce was mortified as some of the questions and answers were so detailed she would *never* have thought to

48

ask them, but her mother, having prepared the wretched thing, was determined to go through each one in excruciating point-by-point detail. It was *months* before Lucy could look her mum and dad in the eye again. Not only that, but Bella had laid out on the kitchen table different examples of contraceptives. Luce says even now when she's sitting at the table she has mental flashbacks of a Dutch cap in the centre of a plate of coloured condoms next to a teacup of M&Ms which were supposed to represent the Pill.

Sorrel claims that she has always just known *everything* on account of her mother having so many children, and because Jasmine was all too willing to give her every possible detail, even making up the bits she didn't know.

With no older siblings and a mother and father who would probably be horrified at Bella Malone's home-made sex manual, I had to pick it all up from teen magazines, so I reckon there are still some *serious* gaps in my knowledge.

No, life seems to be carrying on as before, it's just as if Dad is out at work all the time and Mum is going through confectionery at a faster rate. The only difference seems to be that a couple of suitcases have gone from the cupboard under the stairs, making more room for my shoes and Jack's football boots.

'I *bet* you he's got a girlfriend,' says Sorrel, licking the wrapper of her Chicken Whopper. 'There'll have been signs that he was about to leave. It just you've been too damn blinkered to have noticed them.'

Chapter Five

Could there have been signs? Clues that I have missed? Signals that something was wrong, possibly even that Dad has some tarty totty half his age as a girlfriend? It's hard to know, as I suspect that even if Dad had sat at the kitchen table with a Post-It note stuck to his forehead saying *I'm Off* I probably wouldn't have noticed. In fact, if he hadn't announced he was going, I probably wouldn't have even realized, and just thought he was working late all the time.

Lying on my bed, staring at the ceiling, doubts begin to creep into my mind.

I sit up, grab my moby and ring Sorrel. When she answers she says she's out with her mother slapping *Gas Guzzler* stickers on the windscreens of people carriers and 4x4s, or *Beast Buses and Beast Cars* as Yolanda calls them. Sorrel says she doesn't care about 4x4s, but she goes with her mother because she enjoys seeing people go potty when they find a sticker on their car.

'What am I looking for?' I ask. 'He's taken his laptop so I can't find any incriminating emails.'

I'd snooped through all the paperwork I could find in what Dad always calls *the study*, but is really just a room so small you can't squeeze a single bed in, but instead of steamy love letters, all I found was bills, junk mail and pension plans.

I hear Yolanda yell in the background, 'We're not vandals, we're eco-warriors!'

Sorrel speaks in a rapid whisper. 'You're not after those sorts of clues, more like changes in his behaviour. Think what he was like say a year ago, and how he was just before he left. I bet you'll find *loads* of differences.'

'But will they tell me if he has some hot totty?' I ask her.

'Three minutes!' Sorrel hisses, and the line goes dead.

Sorrel's mum has put a three-minute time limit on her moby. This isn't so that Sorrel doesn't run up huge bills, but because Yolanda is worried that mobile phones fry young brain cells if they're clamped next to your head for longer than three minutes. This means that even if *I* phone Sorrel when her mum is around I can only talk to her for three minutes. It sounds a pain, but in exchange for the Three Minute Warning, Sorrel's mum pays her phone bill.

I've also got a sort of three-minute limit, but it's self-imposed. Dad *used* to pay my bill, but then there was a monstrous triple-figure one. Lucy had gone to France with her mother to get some Home Stylist stuff and I'd *no* idea calling foreign numbers was so expensive. I do now. And now the parentals insist I pay as I go.

My moby vibrates once. A text from Sorrel.

`Any mega blow ups?`

My parents don't row. Dad shouts at Jack and me for doing daft things like the time I left the top off the milk carton by mistake so Dad poured it all over the table and his clean jeans, and Mum is more of a quick snapper than a shouter, say when Jack has forgotten to tell her he needs a clean football kit until he's at the front door on the way to school, but they never seem to shout or snap at each other.

I stab `They never row` on the keypad.

But as I press *Send* I suddenly remember that this isn't true. I was a witness to the Curious Incident of the Peach Stone on the Kitchen Floor.

Whilst Bella Malone is a *place for everything and everything in its place* type of person, the Queen of the Grubs is an *everything on the floor or stuffed in a drawer* type. Mum surrounds herself with stuff. The chaos and clutter never seemed to bother Dad, or at least, I don't remember him complaining that it did, until something odd happened, about a month before Christmas.

Dad came in from work and went to the fridge, probably for a beer. I was half reading *Teen Vogue* on the sofa and half watching *Hollyoaks*, and Mum was sitting at the kitchen table doing a Sudoku puzzle whilst cremating something for tea in the oven. Who knows where The Little Runt was? Suddenly Dad slammed the fridge door shut, marched over to the pedal bin, pulled it out of the corner and snapped, 'Why is there a peach stone on the floor?'

Mum didn't look up from Sudoku but said, 'Oh, it was supposed to go in the bin, but I missed.'

'Then if you *know* you missed the bin, why didn't you bother to pick it up?'

This is another Mother Mystery which has never been solved. Mum will drop things and just leave them on the floor until she drops something else nearby, and *then* she'll bend down and pick both of them up. Single items can remain marooned near the bin or the washing basket for *weeks*. She once dropped a pair of Jack's pants on the top stair on their way down to the washing machine, and it took a *week* for them to gradually move down the stairs until they reached the bottom where they eventually found a stray sock and *then* they got picked up. No, I didn't pick them up. It was an experiment to see how long used pants would take to crawl by themselves into the wash, and I am *not* touching my brother's kegs. They should have a biohazard sticker on them and that tape that says *Police Line Do Not Cross* circling the area, especially as when they reached about the third step from the top, I noticed what looked suspiciously like skid marks inside them. Eeeww!

I used to think that this aversion to picking things up might be something to do with the Mighty Mammaries, that somehow they restricted her from bending over, or that she was scared that if she bent over too far her centre of gravity would pull her towards the floor and she would never get up again. More recently I decided this is unlikely, because I've seen her drop a purple Quality Street, and she was surprisingly quick and agile in the way she swooped down, picked it up, unwrapped it and popped it into her mouth in one smooth movement.

Anyway, when I glanced up from my mag, I noticed Dad had picked up the peach stone and was standing in the middle of the kitchen, brandishing it. It was gross, covered in dust, fluff, hairs and bits of crushed eggshell.

'This has been on the floor for *weeks*!' he said. 'I've been monitoring it!'

That should have been an early sign. Use of the word *monitoring*. Very un-Dad like.

'Why didn't anyone in this family think to pick it up?'

I *think* this question was actually addressed to both of us, but as I hadn't even *noticed* the offending peach stone, I didn't answer. Mum did though. She filled in another Sudoku grid and said calmly and without even a hint of narkiness, 'Well, Rob, if you've been watching it for weeks, why didn't *you* pick it up?'

Dad went potty. *Totally* nuclear. It was as if a volcano of emotion had erupted. He started ranting away, asking if we thought that by leaving a peach stone on the floor we were hoping it might burrow through the tiles and take root in the kitchen, growing into a fully formed peach tree with fruit that we could just pick off whenever we fancied it. 'Are you hoping our basement might turn into a ruddy orchard?' he yelled.

I was going to point out he was being ridiculous, as even if roots from the peach stone *could* force their way through terracotta floor tiles, the sun never makes it into our basement kitchen long enough to ripen the fruit, but he was so mad, so out of control, I decided to keep quiet.

After ranting about the state of the house for what

seemed like ages he yelled, 'I can't stand it any longer!' and stormed out of the kitchen. We heard him slam the front door and zoom off in his van.

'What was all that about?' I asked Mum, who looked a bit ruffled.

'I've absolutely no idea, love,' she said.

And, at the time, we didn't.

I'm not suggesting my dad left my mum just because we left a peach stone festering on the floor for weeks but, looking back, was his totally over-the-top and out-of-character reaction to it a sign that something was wrong?

Did the peach stone topple him over the edge of sanity?

Instead of the final straw, was it the final stone?

Why did he use the word *monitoring*?

Something was odd.

Dad gets annoyed because of work, if say an agency plumber has let him down, or if a shipment of U-bends hasn't arrived. He's been known to go pretty potty over homework or school issues. The Skinners next door letting their leylandii tree grow so big it blocks our light gets him steaming, as does the fact that their huge furry cat, Tiny, comes and craps in our garden but leaves their lawn pristine. But getting stressy-headed over something like a peach stone covered in hair on the floor? Never.

Of course, now I've found one dodgy sign that all was not well, I've thought of *loads* of others.

His Phone

When did Dad start taking his moby out of the room when it rang? He never used to. We'd be sitting down to tea or watching television, his phone would ring, and when he answered it, it would be all, 'Hi, Barry, yes. It'll take twelve metres of ten-millimetre copper pipe and several straight copper solder ring couplings. I'll pop over later and make sure everything's going OK,' and then he'd put the phone down and get on with whatever he was doing when it rang. But then he started leaving the room when the phone went, taking it out into the garden, or even the street. If I went anywhere near him he'd scowl, put his hand over the receiver and hiss, 'Can't you see I'm on the phone?' which is such a daft thing to say, as of course I could *see* he was on the phone, I just didn't realize it was such a problem me being near him when he was.

His Hair

He's become obsessed about the fact that he's going bald and has bought all sorts of hair-restorer-type lotions which haven't worked, but have given him a very flaky scalp. Personally, if I was a man, I'd rather be bald than have rampant dandruff, but as a woman I'd plump for the snow-on-the-shoulder dandruff scenario over the coot-head look every time.

The Pong Factor

Dad isn't an aftershave sort of person. This has always annoyed me as dads are mega problematical on the pressie front, unless they've got a hobby like golf or fly fishing, and then you can buy them a golf club cover shaped like a parrot or pretty feather flies for fishing. Without a hobby, the fallback for difficult dads is always aftershave. But not for my dad. He says as he's spent years sniffing around rank toilets, stinko drains and damp baths, his sense of smell is trashed and aftershave would be a waste of money. But he *was* wearing some on Christmas Day. I know he was. I remember thinking *Mmm, nice pong* when I gave him a hug and a kiss to thank him for the digi camera. But why now and after all these years, and who bought it for him?

His Teeth

This is the *weirdest* thing of all. Dad's had his teeth whitened! He's had to spend a lot of time at the dentist's over the past few months because several of his fillings needed replacing and he'd cracked a crown biting down on a piece of burnt pizza crust. Dad's teeth are really crumbly because Nana Pat let him eat as many sweets as he wanted when he was a kid. Fillings and stuff I can understand (though I'm filling-free!) but the teeth-whitening thing is odd. He *said* that the dentist did it free of charge given that he'd spent so much money on the other stuff, but still . . .

Maybe Sorrel's right. There have been odd things. I'm definitely going to ask Mum whether Dad's left us for someone else. I'll have to choose my place and time carefully, somewhere where Mum won't be able to just get up and walk out, or get upset, or ignore me or pretend she hasn't heard. I'll ask her tomorrow when we're at Grandma and Granddad's for lunch.

Chapter Six

I'm a great believer in asking awkward questions or revealing dodgy information to parents when there are other people about. Safety in numbers and all that. They might want to go bonkers, drag you out of the room and shout at you for doing whatever you've done that they don't like, but they'll be too polite to give you hell in front of someone else. Then, by the time you're on your own with them, some of their molten fury will have been diffused, or so you hope. It's the difference between popping a balloon with a pin, or just letting it go down slowly. A bang as opposed to a whimper. Where parents are concerned, slow controlled release of potentially explosive information is *always* better than a big bang. This might not apply to *really* serious information like you've been expelled for bullying, been caught Happy Slapping, are pregnant or got wasted on alcopops during lessons. Then, you'd probably be given hell even if you were sitting in a church surrounded by strangers, waiting for a funeral to start, but for your everyday, bog-standard type of dodgy info, the system *always* works.

Actual examples of the Controlled Release Information System in action include:

1. Whispering to Mum that I'd got an E in a big school project, just before the curtain went up on *Dick Whittington* when we went to the pantomime last Christmas (just for Jack, you understand; I'm *so* over pantomimes). The crappy grade wasn't entirely my fault, and I'm still miffed that my history teacher, Mr Moxon, didn't accept some responsibility. When Poxy Moxy asked us to do a project on an influential person, and wrote *Influential Person* on the board, he should have been more specific. I chose Hilary Duff (now there's a woman with a perfect-shaped face and an inappropriate surname) because Hils is influential to me, but apparently Poxy meant someone influential to the world, like Hitler or Churchill, not Hilary.

2. Showing Dad the new henna tattoo on my left shoulder – which turned out not to be *quite* as temporary as the little woman on the stall in the market promised – just as Dad's brother, Uncle Richard, walked through the

door with his suitcases on a visit from Edinburgh. I'd had it done in an attempt to deflect attention away from my salami arms but, months later, what was a beautiful butterfly with delicate wings now resembles a giant mouse turd with dotty antennae, the wings having faded away long before the rest of it.

3. Waiting in the dentist's, and *just* before the dentist called out my name, admitting to Mum that I'd failed my chemistry test because I'd thought I was supposed to be revising for a biology exam. I was particularly annoyed because I'd spent at least half an hour learning the names of all the gastric enzymes, but didn't know *anything* about the periodic table.

Anyway, potentially explosive situations, all calmly diffused, or at the very least diminished. So going to the grandparentals is an ideal opportunity smoothly to slip in the question that no daughter ever wants to ask her mum: Has Dad left us for some tarty trollop?

We've spent two hours in the car, pulled into Magnolia Close (a cul-de-sac full of identical neat bungalows), had lunch (quiche Lorraine, salady bits and bananas with squirty cream, OK for summer but odd for early January when it's cold outside), opened our late Christmas presents (a professional football for Jack, a printer to go with my digital camera for me, a scarf I know Mum will never wear), given them theirs (scented lavender drawer-liner paper and bath stuff for Grandma, gardening gloves, a daisy grubber and a book on dahlias for Granddad) and now Mum and I are perched on the gold nylon-velvet-covered sofa whilst Grandma hands out tea and scrummy Mr Kipling Almond Slices. No one has said anything about Dad, and until *someone* mentions *something* I'd feel awkward just popping the trollop question.

What Grandma *has* talked about, endlessly, is their trip to New York to spend Christmas with Aunty Vicky, Uncle Hamp and Madison. She's *full* of it. Poor Granddad. He's in a world of his own and just ignores her. I think it's the only way he can cope with being married to her for almost forty years. She *never* stops rabbiting.

'Of course, Hamp works very hard to give them such a comfortable lifestyle,' Grandma says as she puts down the plate of Almond Slices and begins to hand round a wad of photos. 'Their new apartment on the Upper East Side is *wonderful*. You wouldn't think their flat could be bigger than your house, but it's vast and has an *enormous* roof terrace. Victoria says that she'd find it impossible to live vertically now she's become used to lateral living. Eleanor, I *really* think you should try and make it over there this year. It's been *ages* since you've seen Victoria, and you'd hardly recognize the lovely Madison.'

From the number of photos that Aunty Vicky sends us I think I'd recognize the Goddess Madison anywhere.

As I'm handed some snaps I look closely to see whether my Wundacousin is sporting evidence of emerging Mighty Mammaries. I can't see anything. If she's not holding a trophy, she's standing behind a horse and carriage, throwing her arms around the grandparents, or hugging her Christmas present, a cute red sausage dog puppy who's all wrinkly paws and velvety ears. I *really* envy her that. I'm *desperate* for a pupster, but as I didn't look after Google after the first flush of *Oooh he's so cute!* wore off (and this was way *before* he turned into the pet from hell) Mum doesn't trust me to poop a scoop a dog for the rest of its life.

It had snowed for most of the time they were in New York, so there are photographs of Madison in Central Park making the world's best snowman complete with a perfectly shaped carrot nose. There's another one of her throwing fluffy snowballs towards the camera and several of her just posing in the pristine white snow, looking like a model from Gap adverts in her matching hat, gloves and scarf, but too wrapped up for me to tell what might be lurking underneath her warm-but-oh-so-stylish red coat.

'How is Madison?' Mum asks Grandma, passing me more photos of the Goddess frolicking in the snow. 'I haven't spoken to her or Hamp for ages.'

'Oh, she's the most beautiful girl both in looks and personality,' Grandma gushes. 'And Hamp's financial advice business is booming.' She begins to pour some tea into wafer-thin white and gold china cups. 'As I say, you really should go out there, Eleanor. You, the children and *Robert*.' She curls the word *Robert* around her tongue, saying my dad's name as if he's some kind of bottom-dwelling lowlife, and I look up from the photos to see Grandma pursing her lips and her only slightly-less-large-than-Mum's Mighty Mammaries heaving with indignation. 'It's such a shame he couldn't put himself out to come this afternoon. It's been *ages* since we've seen him.'

'He's been very busy at work.' Mum sounds defensive. 'The new stadium is taking up lots of his time and there's been a problem with installing so many toilets, and somehow he's got involved in an issue with the hand-dryers they want to use, even though *I* think that's really an electrical problem rather than a plumbing issue, and . . .'

I switch off. Mum is gabbling. There's just a continuous *yadda yadda yadda* in the background, until finally Grandma interrupts in her tart uptight voice. 'Well, I'm sorry, Eleanor, but I do think that he could have taken a couple of hours off this afternoon to come and see us. I know you manage to see Patricia regularly.'

I'm still looking at the photos of Madison, holding them up to the light and examining them from all angles to see whether there is boob-evidence when Mum says sharply, 'Mum, you know he has to work. Holidays put a lot of strain on plumbing systems, Christmas and New Year especially. We've not seen much of him recently, and we haven't seen or heard from Rob's mum for ages. She's been in Scotland for Christmas, visiting Richard.'

'But now Dad's living with her.'

Jack had been quietly playing football Top Trumps with Granddad.

I glance at Mum and see that a bright-red flush is spreading from the upper regions of the Mighty Mammaries towards her neck.

Jack throws his cards up into the air and they scatter down on the swirly orange and brown carpet. 'He's left us to live with Nana Pat.'

Mum's cheeks are now crimson.

Grandma gasps and looks as if she's swallowed a wasp whilst sitting on something hot and *very* pointed. Her eyebrows are raised so high they're in danger of disappearing into her grey hairline.

67

There's a stunned silence before Granddad says softly, 'I'm sorry to hear that, Eleanor love.' He moves stiffly out of his brown mock-leather armchair and begins to pick up the scattered Trump cards, handing them back to Jack.

I'm gobsmacked.

I know they're not close, but the Queen of the Clams obviously hasn't even told her parents that her marriage is in trouble.

Mum is driving us home. Jack is asleep in the back of the car and I'm sitting in the front. It's dark. The glinting cat's-eyes in the road stretch ahead of us, and the lights on the dashboard are twinkling. I feel as if I'm sitting in the cockpit of an aeroplane on a runway, until the image of my mother flying a jumbo jet freaks me out.

Mum is staring at the road ahead. A good thing. Far too often when she's driving she'll be looking at people in the street, or things in shop windows, and fail to notice the car in front has stopped suddenly, or a cyclist has pulled out. We've never actually had a crash, but it's been too close too many times for my liking. Mum's not really a car person. Dad always checks the oil and the water and fills the car up with petrol, and Mum just gets in, stretches the seat belt over her Mighty Mammaries, starts the car and drives.

The dark car seems comforting, like a grey cocoon. I know the question I want to ask but I'm afraid I won't like the answer.

It wasn't the right time at Grandma's. After the shock announcement she ordered Mum into the kitchen and I could hear raised voices through the wall. Then Mum stormed into the living room and told us to get our coats and presents as we were leaving. It didn't seem the right time to pipe up, 'Did Dad leave us for some bit of skirt?'

Now seems a good time. There's hardly any traffic on the road, so although there's still the possibility that Mum might drive on to the verge, roll the car over and kill one or all of us, it reduces the chances of crashing into another car and taking some innocent non-family motorist with us.

I look out of the passenger window and mumble, 'Does Dad have a girlfriend?'

Mum says nothing. I've obviously set my mumbling level too low for her to hear. I try again.

'Does Dad have a girlfriend? Is that why he's left home?'

Mum carries on staring ahead, a relief as it had been a slight worry that she might turn to talk to me and career across the road and into the path of an oncoming car, but she laughs my question away. 'Of course not!'

'Are you sure?'

'Of *course* I'm sure.'

'Did you ask him?'

'Yes.'

'And he denied it?'

'Yes.'

As Queen Clam, she's not going to make this easy for me by volunteering information. I'm going to have to prise it out of her.

'So why *has* he left?'

There's a tense silence, and for a moment I think Mum is going to ignore me, but then she says with a heavy sigh, 'For a breather.' Her voice sounds strained and tired, but going to Grandma's always leaves her strung-out and shattered. 'Middle age is a difficult time for men, you know. They start losing their hair . . .'

'*What!* You mean Dad's left us because he's stressed out he's turning into a coot-head?' I'm shocked that he could be so shallow.

'No! No, not just that!'

'Well, what then?'

'Electra, I've told you. Your dad's at a difficult point in his life. They call it a mid-life crisis. Some men go off and buy powerful motorbikes and sports cars . . .'

'What and Dad had his teeth whitened instead?'

'Something like that.'

'When did he tell you?' Now Mum's shell is slightly open I'm going for it. 'Did he tell you before Christmas? Is that why you weren't well? Did you know on Christmas Day? New Year? When?'

Mum says nothing.

'But you must have been shocked,' I persist. 'Not about the teeth-whitening, but him leaving.'

In the gloom I notice Mum grips the steering wheel tighter, but she doesn't say anything. I look closely at her profile outlined against the car window, but as she has a bit of a double-chin issue it's impossible to tell whether there's any tightening of the jaw area. There's too much loose skin floating around her jowls.

'Why didn't you tell Grandma?'

Based on the last few minutes of ignored questions, I don't expect Mum to answer but she says carefully, 'You know how she is, how she feels about your dad. She'll be on the phone to your Aunty Vicky right now. I was just trying to avoid all that fuss because it might blow over very quickly.'

'But—'

'Electra love, your dad just wants some time and space to himself, so that's what we'll give him.' Mum sounds tired and tense and I can tell she's trying to bring my interrogation to an end.

71

I try one last question.

'So do you think he'll come back?'

Mum says nothing, but rams her foot down on the accelerator and we zoom on, into the dark.

Chapter Seven

I am *so* glad to be going back to school.

I never *ever* thought that I'd say that but, after everything that has gone on, school will be welcomingly normal. In fact, on the first day back after the holidays when I would usually be lying in bed working out whether I could get away with having a day off on the pretence of period pains, even though I used that excuse less than a month ago, I'm up, dressed, and at the bus stop, not just on time, but really early. This is *very* odd for me as I like to lie in bed not until the last possible minute, but several minutes *past* that minute. Usually I'm either running for the bus, have missed the bus and am begging Mum for a lift, or I have to miss breakfast, a shower and/or hair washing relying on cereal bars, deodorant and dry shampoo instead.

I regularly contemplate sleeping in my uniform to

save time getting dressed in the morning, but I'm worried that kipping in the hideous green tartan kilt they force us to wear might give me bizarre nightmares about being turned into a giant haggis, where I'm trying to escape from my sheep's-stomach prison before Sorrel devours me.

The first person I see is Claudia Barnes, aka Tits Out. If you could see her standing at the bus stop you'd understand why me, Luce and Sorrel have given her that nickname, not that we ever call her that to her face. Claudia always sits or stands thrusting her chest so far out, her shoulder blades practically touch at the back. It's not even that she has a particularly large chest – though I admit that with my mother as a marker of big boobs, I'm not in a good position to judge relative sizes – it's just that she presents them to everyone as if they are the most interesting thing about her, which, for the boys at our school, they probably are.

There's a rumour, mainly spread by me, that beneath her bra lurks chicken fillets, those bags of silicone stuff that sit by the till at La Senza. Really I've got no idea whether her baps are fake or not as she always manages to get out of showers after games. If you believe the notes she brings in from home, she's had one continuous period for about a year. She doesn't stink of BO or anything because she doesn't actually *do* anything in games to break into a sweat. She just stands around the hockey pitch or the netball court in her little black pleated skirt and green top, presenting her boobs, looking coyly at the boys playing football or cricket. I stand around doing nothing too, but that's because I'm crap at anything sports-related so no one passes me the ball. The worst part of that whole sporty scene is that we have to tie our hair back for games. Without the camouflage of long hair my dish-face looks *huge*, and although I can cover up the salami arms with a sweatshirt, the mottled salami legs and sturdy thighs are on show. No wonder even the most disgusting Zitty Bum Fluff boys in our year ignore me.

Tits Out always hints that where boys are concerned she's gone further than anyone else, which in my case isn't hard. When the French exchange students came over last summer she had a permanent necklace of hickeys, having been neck-sucked by every Froggy Tom, Dick and Harry (Thierry, Jacques et Henri?). It was as if she'd been attacked by a bunch of French vampires. She was so proud of these badges of slaggery, she didn't even *try* to pull up the collar of her shirt or artfully arrange a scarf around her neck to hide them.

Anyway, Tits Out makes out that she's gone all the way, but I'm sure she hasn't because:

The sort of boys that would go all the way with Claudia would tell the whole year and we would have heard about it,

or:

The boy would discover the chicken fillets in her bra and the whole *school* would have heard about it.

What I know for a fact *is* fake is her hair colour, as no one that naturally blonde has eyebrows that dark. She's plucked them into a thin line to minimize the mismatch, but there's always dark dots coming through, as if she's got a line of ants marching above her eyes.

But the most annoying thing about her is the fact that *whatever* you tell her, whatever you've done, she's been there, done it and is wearing the T-shirt.

'How were the hols?' she asks when she sees me.

'First part good, second part crap,' I say, trying to speak to her face, not her chest.

She's got a silver puffy coat on as it's freezing, but her shoulders are still jerked back so that the puffy pillows on the front stick out even more. I have a strong desire to squeeze them, not her boobs, just the puffy lumps.

'How come?' The line of eyebrow ants do a sharp march upwards as she gives me a quizzical look.

I wasn't going to tell her about Dad, she's a terrible gossip, but then I decide that just because Mum has kept it quiet doesn't mean *I* have to and, by telling her, the entire year will know by first break which gets it out of the way.

'Dad left home.'

'Bummer.'

I nod.

'Who's he shagging?'

Why does everyone assume that? I think. *Can't a dad just leave home without sex being involved?*

'No one! He just needs some space. He's at a difficult age, apparently. A mid-life crisis thing.'

'Oh pur-leese! I know all about that old mid-life crisis excuse!' Tits Out snorts and gives me a knowing look. 'That's what my dad said when he left my mum. Turns out he was giving it to some minx at work who's now my stepmonster. I know *all* about excuses.'

You would, I think.

We get on the bus and scramble to the top deck which is a no-go area at this time of day if you don't wear a Burke's green blazer.

Sorrel lives five stops further back, so she's already there, sitting at the back along with Claudia's bezzie, Natalie Price, who we secretly call Butterface because she wears thick greasy yellow make-up to hide her spots. I wonder what everyone calls *me*? Dish Face? The Sturdy

Salami? It doesn't bear thinking about.

Claudia slips into a seat next to Butterface and announces to the top deck, 'Electra's mum and dad split up over the hols.'

'I *know*,' sneers Sorrel, determined not to let people think that Tits Out was the first with the news.

'Too bad,' says Butterface, chewing gum. 'Who's he gone off with?'

'Er, like no one!' I snap. 'Why does *everyone* assume he's gone off with someone?'

'Sor-ree.' Butterface gets her bulging make-up bag out of her school bag, pulls out a mirror and starts piling on more slap. Whatever emotion she's feeling, her face is always totally vacant, like a death mask plastered in Maybelline make-up. 'I was only asking.'

'Sorry, Nat,' I say. 'It's just the whole thing is weirding me out at the mo.'

Butterface shrugs. I feel bad snapping at her. She's OK, even though she wears tons of make-up, is addicted to her hair-straighteners and is best friends with Tits Out. Tits Out isn't horrid, she's just an annoying know-all wannable slag.

As we approach the school Butterface hands Claudia her mirror, Claudia looks in it and *automatically* smiles at her reflection before handing it back. I can't *ever* imagine smiling at myself in a mirror. I put my make-up on using a tiny-weeny handbag mirror so that I just see each part of my face bit by bit, rather than face the horror of the whole thing. I'm always shocked at how different the picture in my head is compared to my face in the mirror, and I automatically recoil at the terrible collision of imagination and reality.

We clatter down the stairs and pile off the bus near the collection of boxy grey flat-roofed concrete buildings that is Flora Burke's Community School, and start streaming through the gates. Lucy's mum always drives her to school and Luce is already waiting for us by the entrance, smiling. It's a dull cold day, but she looks golden, as if a single ray of sunshine is targeting her. If she wasn't my best friend I'd be so overcome with rabid gut-wrenching jealousy I'd hate her.

Sorrel looks around to check Snitchy Jasmine isn't spying on her and, when she's sure the coast is clear, fishes around in her bag, pulls out a Tupperware of sandwiches and tips them into the bin.

'What Fart Food do you have today?' I ask, unhooking the chandelier earrings I wear to and from school, replacing them with fake-diamond studs.

Sorrel wrinkles her nose. 'Mashed aduki beans on pumpernickel. Gross.'

I used to really hate school, and I mean HATE it. Lessons, homework, teachers, mock exams, real exams, projects, *everything*. School just got in the way of worthwhile pastimes like gossiping, shopping and staying in bed. Then I read a magazine article which said that if you hate something you can't change, then change the way you look at it. *Re-framing* they called it. So now I think of school as one big social club with a few lessons thrown in. It's helped the way I feel about school, but it doesn't seem to have done anything for my grades.

Even though I consider school a seven-hour five-day-a-week social club, I'm not in any particular category, nor am I popular or unpopular. I'd say I was sort of middling-popular. I might have been middle-to-high popular because of being friends with Lucy who's considered high-popular material because of looking so blonde, twiggy and gorgeous, but I'm pulled back to middle-popular because of Sorrel, who's low-popular, just because she growls and scowls at everyone.

We don't really have cliques at our school, unlike Queen Beatrice College for brainy snotty-nosed girls. Apparently, at Queen Bee's, if you're not in the popular clique you might as well go out into the road, lie down and wait for a lorry to run you over as your life isn't worth living.

I'm *glad* I failed their entrance exam. Lucy didn't try for QB. Bella wanted her to go to Church Hill where you just need money, not brains, but Lucy cried so much at the thought we might be separated, Bella changed her mind. Sorrel's bright enough to have gone to QB, but her mum doesn't agree with fee-paying education.

At Burke's, we have categories rather than cliques. The difference between a clique and a category is that in a clique if you're seen talking to an out-of-clique girl, particularly one from a lower clique in the clique hierarchy, then you're expelled from the clique and left friendless in the wilderness to consider the death-by-lorry option. In a category system, although you have your groups of friends, and some people you never talk to just because they're freaky creepy losers, there's plenty of cross-category interaction without fear of expulsion and having your legs crushed by an articulated truck.

Broadly speaking, at Burke's the major categories for girls are:

The Sleazers, e.g. Butterface and Tits Out who is the Queen of Sleaze. The Sleazers are not just defined by who they *claim* to have gone all the way with, but how much make-up they wear, how short their skirts are and the length of their French-manicured nails. They usually have a packet of fags and some condoms in their bag, but I'm pretty sure they're only slag accessories, i.e. in there for effect rather than use. Sometimes, when we're hanging around the newsagent's after school and the sixth-form boys turn up, Tits Out will *deliberately* rummage around in her bag, pull out her slag accessories, and just put them back again, and I notice that the packets have *never* been opened.

The Princesses of Cool are girls like Lucy who always have the right hair and clothes, and look as if they are just passing time at school until they're spotted by a model agency scout, or a footballer who'll marry them and whisk them off to live in a large house with a heart-shaped indoor pool, a home cinema and a spread in *Hello!* magazine.

The Sporty set spend all their time hurtling around netball courts and hockey pitches, and just because they're so busy with matches and fixtures, tend not to have the time to speak to the athletically challenged.

The Geeks practise Geekology by *never* wearing make-up, *always* having sensible shoes even for out of school, and would rather *die* than be seen reading trashy mags. They spend all their free time in the computer suite or having extension lessons in maths and physics as the rest of us can't keep up with their turbo-charged brains. They're useful when you haven't done your homework and need someone to give you the right answers, as with one jab of a manicured nail in their direction they stammer and sweat and hand over their work.

The boys don't fit into quite the same categories, as for reasons which I think are *totally* unfair they are *never* called Sleazers, *however* many girls they *claim* to have gone with. Sporty boys are immediately cool, therefore two categories merge into one, the Spoolios, and there are three times as many Geek boys as girls.

The Zitty Bum Fluff boys need no explanation.

And then there is Freak Boy.

Yes, if it wasn't for lessons, going to school would be a blast.

I limp through registration with Frosty the Penguin (couldn't Mr Frosty at least have bought his wife a new cardigan for Christmas, one in a colour other than black?), a period of maths with a nameless supply teacher who seems unsure of what year he is supposed to be teaching, history with Poxy Moxy, and then after break an hour of geography.

We have a new geography teacher this term. He's tall, young, has floppy blond hair, is *very* good-looking, and from the look of his neat muscly butt when he turns to write his name on the board – Jon Butler – he obviously works out. Mr Butler is a Burke's Virgin, this is his first lesson here, and it's obviously his first full-time teaching post. You can tell the new teachers because in the first few weeks they're all bright-eyed and bushy-tailed, eager to excite the bunch of glassy-eyed pupils sitting in front of them with the subject they've studied at university. By half-term they're drinking a bottle of red wine every night whilst marking books, and by the end of the year, they're at the doc's begging for Prozac and a sick note.

'I know that some of you find geography dry and boring,' Mr Butler says, flashing a cute smile as I mentally start to assign him a score on the Snogability Scale. 'But it doesn't have to be like that. Think of yourself as a detective in a global mystery. The landscape can give you clues . . .'

'Buff Butler is a 3.9 verging on a 4, and that was a *very* interesting lesson,' I say to Lucy and Sorrel as we stand in the lunch queue. 'It's given me an idea for a cunning plan.'

The girls look as if they're going to faint with shock at the phrase *very interesting lesson* coming out of my mouth.

I ignore their looks of mock horror. 'All that stuff about investigating the geographical evidence has made me realize what I need is a private detective.'

'Why?' Lucy takes a tray and passes one to me.

Sorrel doesn't take a tray. Because she bins her Fart Food, she's worried that Jasmine will see her snarfing burgers and report home (as a year-eleven prefect she sometimes supervises the lunch queue), and because she wants to keep all her money for meaty trips to Burger King and KFC, Sorrel doesn't buy lunch but pinches things off our plates, particularly Lucy's as Luce *never* finishes a meal. Perhaps it's flashbacks to the birthday contraceptive buffet her mother laid on that's permanently wrecked her appetite.

'Duh! To find out whether my dad has a girlfriend,' I say. 'Keep up.'

We inch towards the front of the queue.

'Oh, Electra, don't torture yourself,' says Lucy choosing a ham salad.

'*You* said you were sure he didn't,' adds Sorrel.

'I am,' I say, grabbing a slice of pepperoni pizza and holding out my plate for chips. 'I just need to prove it.'

As we're waiting to pay, Freak Boy suddenly appears at my shoulder. That's one of the many weird things about Freak Boy. He's a lurker. A *silent* lurker. You don't know he's there until he comes out with one of his stupid facts or snippets of useless information, and then you wonder *How long has he been lurking?* He gives me the freako creepos.

'I hear your mum and dad have split up,' he says in his squeaky droney testosterone-devoid voice. He doesn't look at me. He never looks at anyone. He *always* has his shoulders hunched and his head down.

'What's it to you?' I say, turning away.

I can't believe that Tits Out would have told him. Even *she* couldn't bring herself to interact with him. He must have overheard her telling someone else when he was lurking.

'I thought you'd like to know that more divorce petitions are lodged in the period just after Christmas and New Year than at any other time. From the figures I've seen, about twenty per cent of divorce petitions begin in January alone.'

'Oh, get lost,' I say, handing over my money.

Freak Boy ignores my instruction and continues to hover beside me.

'I just thought it might help to know that hundreds of kids will be going through the same thing as you, right now.'

'She said, get lost,' snarls Sorrel, trying to grab a piece of pepperoni off the top of my pizza slice. I slap her hand. I don't mind sharing my lunch with her, but I do wish she'd wait until we've sat down.

Freak Boy scuttles off to wherever freaky beetle

losers sit to munch their lunch, and we flop down at a table.

'I'm being serious,' I say. 'I need a private eye. Someone who can follow Dad and give me a report back on his movements. I'm *sure* he doesn't have a girlfriend, but I need to prove it and shut Miss Know-It-All-Tits-Out up for good.'

Sorrel nicks a chip from my plate. 'How are you going to find one?'

'The phone book, the Internet, I dunno. I haven't thought about *specifics*.'

'And how are you going to afford one?' Sorrel takes *another* chip and waves it in the air. 'They'll charge by the hour, and if you want them to follow your old man all day, you'll need about twelve hours.' She pops the chip in her mouth with one hand and reaches for another with the other. 'Even at the minimum wage, and it'll be tons more than that, you're looking at,' she rolls her eyes back trying to do the maths, 'I don't know, but *wads* of wonga.'

Sorrel notices that Lucy has put her knife and fork down, leaving a whole piece of ham, a bit of lettuce and most of the tomato. 'You finished with that?' she asks. Lucy nods and Sorrel leans over and grabs the ham. She tries to put the whole piece in her mouth at once and ends up slapping her face with the luminous pink slice.

'*De-licious*,' she says, licking her lips and then her hand.

'So, what am I going to do?' I say.

'Ask him?' suggests Lucy, and I give her a *Are you completely off your rocker?*-type look.

'OK, what about following him yourself?' she says.

'Yeah, right!' I laugh. 'I think he's going to notice me following him, and anyway, how would I keep up? I can't drive and I am *not* riding a bike.' I haven't put my bum on a saddle since the days when I scooted around on a pink Barbie bike with silver glitter streamers tied to the handlebars. It wasn't the bike, but when I was older and cared about such things, I caught sight of myself in my shiny pink helmet looking like a throbbing zit, and *instantly* that was the end of my cycling days.

'What you need,' says Sorrel, 'is someone your old man doesn't know, someone who'll look for the smallest detail and is happy to spend time lurking about the place, for free.'

It's the word *lurking* that does it. The three of us swivel our heads around. We spot him. Sitting on his own a few tables away from us, hunched over a magazine.

'Hey, FB! Over here!' Sorrel yells.

Freak Boy thinks we call him FB because his name is Frazer Burns. We'd *never* call him Freak Boy to his face.

We might be bitchy, but we are *not* bullies, though sometimes I think Sorrel gets very close to being one with her sarky remarks and cutting put-downs.

Freak Boy glances under his greasy fringe to see Sorrel gesturing to him to come over to our table.

'Do we have to . . .?' I begin, as FB scuttles towards us.

'Leave it to me,' Sorrel hisses.

'Do you want the source of the divorce statistics I gave you?' asks FB, his face flushing so that his nose resembles a beaky beacon. 'I'm sure I can track down the reference quite quickly.'

'Forget that,' says Sorrel. 'How do you fancy doing something for Electra?' She makes her voice go all low and husky. 'Doing something she *really really* wants? Doing something that will please her? Something nobody else can do as well as you.'

Her voice sounds *very* dirty.

Freak Boy goes puce. I'm sure I'm pretty pink too.

'Er . . . well . . . yes,' he squeaks. 'Anything.'

'Good!' exclaims Sorrel triumphantly. 'Over to you, Electra.'

I gulp. 'I need someone to follow my dad for a day. I need to find out whether he's left us for someone else. A *woman*,' I emphasize, just in case FB gets any funny ideas. 'He's denied it, but I need to make sure. You'll need to do it during the week as it might be one of the women at his office or a desperate housewife.'

'I'll do it,' says FB. His face is extra creepy when he looks eager. 'During half-term.'

'Half-term!' I snap at him. 'We've only just come back after the holidays. I can't wait until half-term!'

'If he hasn't got a tart now, he will by then,' says Sorrel darkly. 'And it will be all *your* fault, FB!' She bites a chip in half in a very aggressive way and Freak Boy looks flustered.

'Well, I suppose I could pretend to be ill and sneak out of the house,' he says. 'Mum works nights some weeks and days on others, so I could pretend to be ill on one of the days.'

'Then do it!' urges Sorrel, jabbing half a chip at him.

Freak Boy starts warming to his task. 'I'll need a photo of the suspect,' he says, 'and details of where he works, where he's living, his car and so on.'

'He's not a suspect, he's my dad!' I'm beginning to regret involving the Freak. 'I'll get you those things.'

'You could email them to me,' says Freak Boy. 'Or you could give me your address and I'll come round.'

The moment he says it he knows he's overstepped the mark. Addresses, either email or home, are for friends, not freaks.

'As if!' I say, horrified. 'Give me your address and I'll get them to you.'

'And when you've done that,' orders Sorrel, 'go and buy me a plate of chicken nuggets.'

Chapter Eight

When I get home from school I have the shock of my life.

Mum is standing in front of the television exercising along to a DVD. I say exercising, she's really just moving her arms around and shrugging her shoulders whilst the Mighty Mammaries are bobbing about, up and down, left and right, as if they're doing a *completely* different exercise routine.

'Hi, Mum!' I say, picking up the DVD case. *Pilates with Fern Britton.*

I peer closer at the TV. Having the MM gene certainly doesn't stop Fern from exercising, and she looks fab, but I guess she wears a better bra than Mum. 'What's with the DVD?'

'I thought it was about time I did something about my weight,' says Mum, huffing and puffing along with Fern.

'It's crept up since Jack was born and I've been feeling a bit slow and stodgy recently.'

I'm amazed. Mum *never* talks about the fact that she's a bit of a porker. It's another one of the great Brown family unmentionables.

'What's that smell?' I say, sniffing the air. It's a nasty bitter smell, and I wonder if Mum has overdone the exercising and underdone the deodorant.

'Cabbage,' she replies, giving a final mighty fling of her arms. 'From today I'm on a cabbage soup diet.' She stops the DVD and turns to me, pink in the face and flushed across her chest. 'Just to kick-start the weight loss.'

I'm so surprised I can't think of what to say other than, 'What's for tea?'

'Cabbage soup for me, but lasagne, salad and oven chips for you. It's going to be a bit later tonight as Jack's got five-a-side football at the sports centre, and then an extra half-hour of shooting practice. Oh, and your dad's already been round and fed Google, but he might like some extra cabbage leaves.'

I presume she means the guinea pig, not Dad.

'I'll stuff some leaves through the cage, and then I've got homework to do,' I say. It sounds better than admitting *I'm going to my room to print off a photo to give to*

Freak Boy so he can stalk Dad and I can prove to everyone he's not got a mistress stashed away.

I can't escape the smell of cabbage. It's on my hands from the leaves I gave to Google, and has risen to the top of the house and into my room. I try to mask the pong by spraying perfume about, but the smell of cabbage mixed with Anaïs Anaïs proves a toxic combination, and I end up coughing and having to hold my pillow over my face until the droplets of perfume mixed with cabbage stench have settled. When I think it's safe to come out from behind the pillow I open my knicker drawer, stuff my hands under piles and piles of underwear, and pull out my new digital camera wrapped in a pair of horrid old navy knickers, relics from primary school when we had to prance around in our underwear to something called *Music & Movement*. The knicker disguise is to stop The Little Runt from 'borrowing' my camera to take snaps of his toy Dalek before the Dalek exterminates it for taking a picture. He wouldn't *dare* look in my knicker drawer. I've told him that if he does I'll put a curse on Arsenal so that all their players will end up with broken legs.

I start to flick through the photos in the viewer, but decide as I'd edited the duff ones as I went along, I might as well just print them all out. I pull the memory card out of the camera, slot it in to the printer, press *Print All* and away it goes, slowly spewing out my snaps while I start to get changed out of my prison uniform.

I pick the first photo out of the tray. It was taken just after I'd unwrapped the camera. Mum is sitting at one end of the sofa with a huge tin of Quality Street resting on her boob-shelf. She's trying to smile but it's a bit of a crooked grin. I remember I'd taken the photograph just after she'd popped one of the big flat gold penny toffees into her mouth, so I thought that's why she was looking odd. Those toffees can be lethal to the dentally challenged. Granddad's false teeth stuck together when he tried one the Christmas before. He had to take his teeth out and chip bits of toffee off them with a penknife to separate the top and bottom plates. Now he sticks to the soft green triangles. Was Mum's lopsided smile because of the toffee on her teeth, or was she trying to put a brave face on the fact that she knew Dad was having a mid-life crisis?

Perched at the other end of the sofa, on one of the arms, Dad doesn't look as if he's in mental turmoil, though even on Christmas Day he's clutching his moby. Was he expecting a call?

In between them is Jack, holding up the Arsenal scarf someone had bought him, pulling a stupid face. The Little Runt does that all the time. The *moment* a camera is pointed in his direction he sticks his tongue out, or screws his face up, or pulls his ears out. He even did it for the school photo, putting his fingers up his nose. *That* didn't go down well with Grandma when Mum sent her a copy.

I look through the others as they slowly churn out.

A shot of the Christmas tree which was droopy by Christmas Day as we'd insisted it went up on the 1st of December, and then forgotten to put any water in the bucket.

Several pics of Dad looking up a giant Dalek's bottom, trying to find out where to put the batteries.

A few snaps of Mum in the kitchen stuffing the turkey with one hand and waving with the other.

Then there's a picture of Christmas lunch.

I peer closely at the photo, still damp from the printer. When I took it we were just about to start eating. The table is full of food, our plates are piled high. Mum and Jack are wearing paper hats and holding up glasses of wine and Ribena. Mum is smiling. Jack has put two roast parsnips up his nose. But Dad's place is empty. His chair is pushed back, his green paper hat tossed on the table along with the pulled cracker. Just as I was about to take the picture his mobile phone had rung and he'd gone into the garden to take the call, only to come back in and say there was a plumbing emergency and he had to go out. I remember Mum saying something like, 'Oh, Rob, *please*, *not* on Christmas Day!' and Dad saying crossly, 'Well, I can charge triple time. There's extra pressure on plumbing systems during the holiday. Some pipes are having to cope with four times the volume of raw sewage they usually do.' *Not* what you want to hear when you are about to tuck into turkey with all the trimmings.

I don't know what time he came back. The three of us spent the rest of the day slumped in front of the TV, snacking on leftovers and smashing open Terry's Chocolate Oranges with Christmas books.

I push the sofa photo into an envelope, along with a bit of paper on which I've scribbled down the address of Dad's office, Nana Pat's maisonette, written *Blue and White Transit van with large plunger painted on side*, and printed *Attention: F B* on the envelope. Then I put my camera back in its knicker nest, close the drawer, go downstairs, and put my head round the kitchen door. Mum is chopping *more* cabbage. The house is turning into a giant cabbage patch.

'I'm nipping out,' I say. 'Just to deliver something to a house in Compton Avenue. I won't be long.'

* * *

I've chosen what to wear with great care. It may be dark, but it still doesn't pay to take any chances of being recognized either coming or going to Freak Boy's house.

I've adopted a camouflage outfit of black tracksuit bottoms, scrotty trainers that used to light up in the dark but are now so old they've lost their glow, one of Dad's old grey jumpers that I'd borrowed because I was cold but too lazy to go upstairs and get my own and then kept, and one of Jack's woolly hats with Arsenal across the front, which I pull down over my ears as it's cold.

Compton Avenue isn't far from Mortimer Road, but the houses are detached with long gravel drives, rather than semi-detached with no driveway, like ours. I'm surprised that Freak Boy lives in such a posh road, and I double-check the address he's given me. It's not that I expected him to live in a kennel, but 7 Compton Avenue is a *very* nice house. I pause by the gate, wondering whether I'll be able to leg it up the drive, stuff the envelope in the letterbox and hare back down and out into the road without being spotted by Freak Boy. I bet he's *lurking* somewhere behind a curtain, or worse, in the bushes. I do *not* want any interaction with him. He's been hired to do a job, that's all. A job with no pay. Not even the minimum wage. More fool him.

I decide *not* to run up the drive, as a figure dressed in

dark clothes running towards the door of a posh house might attract attention from nosy neighbourhood-watch curtain-twitching types with shotguns, so I opt to creep up the side by the bushes instead. All is going well until I *almost* get to the front door, when a security light comes on, flooding the drive with bright, white light. A dog barks from inside. I panic and try to ram the envelope through the letterbox, only to be met on the other side of the door by frenzied snapping and snarling. Through the frosted half-glass I can see a dog throwing itself at the door like some mental muppet, bouncing up and down, bearing its teeth. As I try to pull the envelope back out, the dog manages a monster bounce and sinks its fangs into the envelope, holding on for dear life. The canine hoodlum is winning the tug of war, so I decide to abandon the envelope and make a run for it. I can print out another photo another day. But just as I let go another light goes on, the front door opens and a man stands in the doorway holding mental muppet dog by the collar in one hand, and with the mangled envelope in the other.

'I'm so sorry,' he says, smiling. 'We had a cage for post on the front door, but it fell off and I haven't got round to putting it back on.'

Muppet dog looks cute now it's stopped snarling, and

has started wagging its tail so hard its entire body is swinging left and right.

This man can't *possibly* be Freak Boy's father. He looks normal. Not just normal but nice. *Hot* nice.

'Was it my son you were after?'

I am shocked that:

A. He refers to Freak Boy as his son,

and

B. That he would automatically think that someone like me, even someone with a satellite-dish face, might visit him!

Then I remember how I'm dressed and what my dish-face must look like topped with a woolly football hat. Freak Girl.

Perhaps I *have* got the wrong house and FB lives next door. Maybe Hot Dad has a Hot Son about to bound down the stairs towards me and I'm dressed like a tramp. Typical!

Freak Boy appears behind his father. Framed in the front door with the light around him and his hot breath coming out into the cold night air like shots of steam, he really does look like an alien emerging from his pod. *Nothing* like his dad. I wonder if I can own up to Sorrel and Lucy that I think FB's father is hot? It's pretty sick to fancy your friend's dad, but as Freak Boy is not a friend, perhaps I can admit to thinking that Mr Burns could, if either I was years older or he was years younger, do very well on the Snogability Scale, possibly a 4.0 or even a 4.1.

'I was just trying to deliver something,' I mutter, 'but I think your dog has eaten it.'

Hot Dad hands Freak Son the butchered envelope. 'I'll just take Archie inside,' he smiles, dragging the wagging dog away from the door, 'and leave you to it.'

I don't like the way he says, 'leave you to *it*'. *It* sounds rather too vague and possibly racy. Hot Dad is probably hiding behind a door right now with Mrs Freak Boy, whispering, 'Finally our unfortunate son has made contact with another alien species. A girl!'

'Do you want to come in?' says FB. 'The light is very bright. It's a 500-watt halogen bulb.'

'No,' I say, before adding, 'Thanks.'

FB nods. I don't think he expected me to say *Yes*. I doubt any girl will ever say *Yes* to Freak Boy.

'I'd better just make sure that the photo is OK,' he says, opening the tooth-marked and dog-slobber-covered envelope. 'I'll need a good likeness.'

It's photo carnage. Jack, once in the middle of the photo, has been obliterated by teeth marks. Mum is just about recognizable at one end of the photo, even though her face is a bit mangled. Dad, on the other end, is hanging on by a thin strip of photo paper.

I want to cry at this image of destruction, not just of a photo, but of a family. *My* family. As the tears prick the back of my eyes I keep my head down and mumble, 'When are you going to do it?'

'Mum's on a two-week night rota now but she'll be back to days soon. I'll follow him on my new mountain bike. I got it for Christmas. It's got twenty-four gears.'

'Thanks,' I say, and crunch my way back down the gravel drive.

I can feel tears springing from the corner of my eyes, but I *so* don't want FB to see me snivel. The security light is still on and 500 watts is *very* bright, so I keep my head down going through the gate and slam straight into two boys wheeling their bikes.

'Hey!' A surprised voice.

'Watch it!' An angry voice.

'Oh, it's you.' A disappointed voice.

I've slammed into not just any two boys, but James Malone and Jags, The Spanish Lurve God. I would rather have run back up the drive and thrown myself into the snapping jaws of mental muppet dog, even if Freak Boy was there, rather than this. I've been so careful to make sure that whenever I've been round at Lucy's and there's even a remote chance of a sighting of Jags, I've got clean hair, face-lengthening dangly earrings and as much make-up as I dare without looking as caked as Butterface. And now I'm in dreggy clothes, with watery eyes and a tea cosy on my head.

'Sorry,' I mumble, praying that at this very moment a land-drain under the pavement will collapse and swallow me up.

'It's a friend of my kid sister's,' explains James.

Even though I've been around before when James has been with Jags, I obviously require an explanation. Although I've got mixed feelings about my name, I *so* wish that James would use it. I also wish he wouldn't refer to me as his kid sister's friend. The way he says it sounds *so* demeaning, as if I'm young enough still to be wearing nappies, and accessorizing with a well-placed bib and dummy.

Jags says nothing, but just looks bored, Spanish, gorgeous and totally deserving of being at the top of my S-Scale.

'Who lives there?' James asks, nodding towards the bright lights of 7 Compton Avenue.

'Dunno,' I shrug, contemplating whether to take the tea cosy off my head, or whether this will reveal a worse horror, hat-flat hair. I opt to keep the hat on. At least it has a footballing theme, so it might have some appeal to sporty Jags.

'I thought you came out of there,' persisted James. 'She did, didn't she?' he asks Jags who just shrugs.

Jags has never said a word directly to me, unless you count the earlier 'Watch it!' when he didn't know it was me who'd slammed into him. I'd like to think this is because he's so dazzled by my beauty it renders him mute (hah!) but I think it's just because he feels I'm not worth the effort of filling his lungs with air for. To Jags, I am a non-person.

'Oh, I did, because I had to deliver something,' I squeak. 'But I don't know who lives there.'

'It's that weird boy with the beaky nose and scuttly beetle walk. I've seen him go in,' Jags says to James. His voice is low and gravelly, light years and several shots of testosterone away from Freak Boy's uncontrollable squeaky squawk.

The security light on the drive goes off and we're lit only by the moon and a gloomy street lamp. I bet I look ghostly in this half-light, dressed in dark colours. Not so much dish-face as moon-face.

'Are you going out with Beaky Beetle Boy?' James teases.

'No! No!' I gasp. I don't want Jags to think that I'd even *look* at Freak Boy in that way. 'I'd never, I mean, I couldn't, how could . . .'

James interrupts. 'The lady doth protest too much, methinks,' he says to Jags, and the two of them dissolve into fits of laughter, and carry on wheeling their bikes down the street, without even saying goodbye.

Chapter Nine

Next day, during first break, standing between the science block and the main school to try and get out of the biting wind, I pump Lucy for info.

'What does he mean about me protesting too much?' I ask. I was so panicked by Jags seeing me in tramp mode, I wasn't sure I'd heard properly.

'Did he say, "The lady doth protest too much, methinks"?' she asks.

'That's it!' I cry. '*That's* what Jags said.'

'It's from *Hamlet*,' says Lucy. 'They're doing Shakespeare at school. James is always wandering around the house saying it. I think it's the only quote he knows other than "To be or not to be, that is the question". He thinks he's being smart, or funny, or both. I think he's just being a prize prat.'

'But what does it mean?'

'I think it means that you're going so over the top saying that something isn't true, it must be.'

'Duh?' I'm still being a total slug-head.

'He thinks you're going out with Freak Boy.'

I groan. This is *terrible*. Not only do I bump into The Spanish Lurve God dressed as a tramp, but now he thinks I'm going out with the world's most unfortunate boy. He's *never* going to look at me now. I'm used goods, tainted by creepy freakery.

'When he came in, did James say he'd seen me?' I ask. Lucy shakes her head.

'Did he say that Jags had said *anything* about me?'

'I've just told you. James didn't say *anything* about meeting you. Your name didn't even crop up.'

'Not even that they bumped into a daggy girl with a tea cosy on her head coming out of Freak Boy's house on Compton Avenue?' I thought I'd try *everything* to jog Lucy's memory.

'Nada. Zero. Zilch. Nothing,' shrugs Lucy. 'Sorry.'

'All right, don't rub it in!' I'm miffed that I'd been so instantly forgettable to both of them. 'What were they doing pushing their bikes anyway?'

'Someone nicked their lights from outside the sports centre,' she replies. 'James went ballistic as he'd only just bought new batteries. He banged on about it all evening.'

'Oh gr-reat!' I say dramatically. 'So he'll come home and complain about petty crime, but he doesn't think to mention that he bumped into me. Well, thanks very much James *Selfish* Malone!' I'm half laughing and half being serious.

'Do you want me to make something up to make you feel better?' Lucy's in fits of giggles. 'Even if it's not true?'

'Yes, please,' I say, pulling a pouty face on purpose.

'OK. What about, James came flying into the house last night and said Jags had fallen madly in love with you, and unless you were prepared to say that you would be his for ever and ever, he was going to flunk his GCSEs on purpose, and live in a cave, eating beetles and drinking rainwater. How's that?'

'Perfecto!' I say, creasing over with laughter.

I suddenly realize it's the first time since the 2nd of January that I have really laughed and it feels *fantastico*. It's as if a weight has been lifted from my meaty henna-tattooed shoulders. I feel normal again. Normal isn't spending time lying on your bed in a house which reeks of decaying cabbage, wondering whether your dad has a behind-the-scenes trollop or is ever coming home. Normal is spending time with your friends, endlessly obsessing over really important issues such as:

Hair: Length (me), colour (me), texture (Sorrel who

one minute has braided hair, then relaxed, then back to braids and so on), fringe or no fringe (me)?

Body Shape: Too big (me), Salami limbs (me), what *hasn't* happened in the boob department (me), what *might* happen in the boob department (me AGAIN)

Face: Everything – (me)

Nails: Me and Sorrel.

Boys: Lucy and me. Sorrel doesn't do boy obsession and only ever gives a maximum score of 1.6 on the S-Scale.

Shopping: Me and Sorrel. Lucy is a clothes-shopping voyeur. She watches but she doesn't take part, though she will buy accessories such as masses of bracelets which she wears all at once.

Add in gossiping/bitching about friends, enemies, music, celebrities and just dissing random strangers walking by on the street, and you've got a great life!

I feel so ordinary, so normal, so free of crap, I decide to let Lucy in on my guilty secret, especially as Sorrel has obviously found something better to do in first break than huddle against a wall with us.

'Don't tell Sorrel or she'll think I've had some sort of a parental-break-up-induced breakdown, but Freak Boy's dad is *really* hot,' I giggle. 'I saw him the other night when I went round there. Luce, I tell you, he's at least a 4.0 on the scale. Maybe even a 4.1!'

'No!' shrieks Lucy. 'No! Not better than Buff? I thought you said you hadn't ventured into the alien pod?'

'I didn't! I saw him on the drive.'

'Well then,' says Lucy, 'it would have been too dark for a true S-rating. He's probably off the scale in the light.' She sounds relieved.

I shake my head. 'A 500-watt halogen bulb lit him, and I tell you, Luce, he was one Hot Dad.'

'FB *must* be adopted,' Lucy decides. 'Or perhaps he was swapped at birth by mistake because the hospital tagged the wrong baby. Hot Dad *can't* share a gene pool with Freak Boy if he's as hot as you say.'

If this *is* the case, I momentarily feel sorry for Hot Dad's biological child being brought up surrounded by a family of beaky freaks, and for Hot Dad to be saddled with a genetic deviant as his son. Then I bask in the fact that I am back to my usual gloriously bitchy self. Yes, life is back to normal and life is *fantastico*!

Chapter Ten

It's Saturday morning.

Dad has popped round, taken Mum's car to the garage to fill it up and left again. He's always popping round to do bits and pieces, but he never stays long.

Jack is on his own in the garden playing football, kicking a ball at the fence which will probably get Mr Skinner looking over and shouting at him to stop as it's making the fence really wobbly. I don't think it's just the ball crashing against the fence which is loosening it. Their monster moggy running up and down it all the time has to take some responsibility.

Mum is loading the washing machine.

This is a more regular occurrence than when Dad was at home. Then, there would be a football shirt here, a pair of trackie bottoms there, and pants *everywhere*. Now Mum seems to be doing washing all the time. And tidying. The house is not exactly spotless, she's not really moved on to *serious* cleaning, but the first impression when you walk in the door is that the house is tidy. Even *I've* flashed the handheld Dustbuster around a bit, just to show some support on the housework front.

I've just spent half an hour giving myself a DIY pedi (soaked, shaped, buffed, pink toe separator – the whole caboodle) and am lying on the sofa in the kitchen, waving my feet in the air, waiting for Cherry Soda (brighter on the toes than in the bottle) to dry. On Saturdays I'd usually be going to Eastwood Circle Retail Park with Lucy and Sorrel for a mooch around the shops, but Luce is going up to London with her parents to take Michael back to uni, and Sorrel is lumbered with looking after Senna and the twins as Ray is doing a Saturday shift in the camera shop. Jasmine has a Saturday job in New Look, but never seems to be around to sibling-sit *whatever* day of the week it is, something else that sends Sorrel into anger orbit.

'Pop upstairs, love, and see if Jack's left anything on the floor that should be in the washer, can you?' Mum asks.

'Why can't he come in and get his own washing?' I moan, not moving.

'He's in the garden,' Mum replies.

'But I've just done my toes!' I flap my feet around to demonstrate.

'Don't give me a hard time!' Mum laughs. 'And since when did you pick up washing with your toes? Go on.'

'OK. But no pants. I won't touch his pants without a chemical suit and gloves.' I still feel mentally scarred by the memory of the skid marks.

As I drag myself off the sofa I give a deep, heavy sigh so Mum knows I'm doing this under protest, and go upstairs really carefully, on my heels, in case Cherry Soda gets smudged on the green Axminster.

From behind Jack's closed bedroom door, I can hear 'Ex-ter-min-ate! Ex-ter-min-ate!'

I take a deep breath, ignore the handwritten *No Entry Electra* sign stuck to the door, and open it.

Jack's room has always reeked of damp gym kit, stale mud and smelly farts but, mixed with lingering cabbage pong, it penks so badly I have to pull my polo-necked jumper over my nose as a makeshift gas mask.

On the floor, his Christmas Dalek has been left switched on, screeching out its instructions of doom. I bend down to turn it off, and when the Dalek has stopped exterminating I hear shouting coming from outside. I look through the window to see Old Man Skinner next door, standing on a chair, hanging over the fence, jabbing his finger at Jack, telling him off for using the fence for footie practice. I'm alarmed to see Jack giving the grey-haired old man a V-sign before running towards the back door.

On the floor is a football magazine. Football isn't really my thing, though these guys look so fit it might be worth trying to get into it, and then I'd be all knowledgeable about the offside rule which might impress boys in general and Jags in particular. I pick up the magazine. Me and the girls can use the S-Scale on the footballers.

There's a noise on the stairs.

'Watch my toes!' I shriek, letting the woolly gas mask slip off my nose as Jack bursts in. 'Keep away, you little runt! Keep away!'

'What are you doing in my room?' he demands, his face flushing beety red with rage. 'Can't you read? You're not allowed in here. Get out, Poo Head!!'

'*Mum* sent me in,' I say primly, parental-derived instructions always carrying more weight. 'She wanted me to *spy* on you. Good job too. You'd left the Dalek on. The batteries would have gone flat.'

'*So*, I've got lots more.' Jack looks defiant and gives me the same V-sign he'd given to Mr Skinner, jabbing his fingers up and down in front of my face.

I decide to take him down a peg or three.

'Mum says take your smelly washing downstairs and clean Google's cage without wearing the oven glove.' This hadn't actually been mentioned, but I thought I'd frighten him just for the hell of it. 'And if you don't, I'll put a curse on the Arsenal team coach so it crashes!'

Jack looks horrified and even *I'm* a bit shocked that I could think of such a horrible thing to say, but before I can feel guilty Jack sees the magazine I'm holding.

'That's new!' he shouts. 'Give it me back, Poo Head!'

He tries to snatch it out of my hand, but I'm taller than him, so just to wind him up I hold it high above my head. He looks down at my glossy toes and tries to stamp on them, but I manage to jump out of the way before staggering backwards and falling on to his bed. But instead of a soft landing, it feels lumpy, as if I've fallen on to a heap of broken bricks.

'What have you got under here?' I snap, jumping up and throwing back the dinosaur duvet. Lying on the crumpled blue sheet is a pile of bicycle lights and batteries.

'Where did you get these?' I hiss.

Jack looks pale. 'I . . . I . . . found them,' he stutters. 'Sort of.'

'You nicked them, didn't you? From bikes at the sports centre.'

Jack nods.

'Did you nick any after shooting practice last week?'

Jack nods again.

I wonder which one belonged to Jags. If I knew, I'd keep it as a souvenir and sleep with it under my pillow. Even though it would make the pillow lumpy and uncomfortable and I wouldn't get much sleep, it would be worth it. Sleeping with his bike lights is probably the closest I'll ever get to him.

'Don't you think Mum already has enough on her plate,' I say shaking him by the shoulders, 'without you turning into a thieving little scroat?'

Jack hangs his head and I feel sorry for him, but not for long.

'I won't tell Mum, but you are *never, ever* to do this again or I'll puncture your new football with my nail scissors. Understand me?'

Chapter Eleven

'Frazer Burns?' Frosty the Penguin squawks out during registration.

There's silence.

'Anyone seen or heard from Frazer today?'

No one says anything.

I feel my stomach turn into a knot.

FB said it would be a couple of weeks before he could bunk off school. Pretend to be ill while his mum went to work. It looks like today is the day. S-Day. Snooping Day. Stalking Day. Surveillance Day. *Spying* Day.

I've had a few reservations since Sorrel forced Freak Boy into helping me, but even though life has got back to normal I still want to put my mind at rest that Dad hasn't got a girlfriend so that I can stop Claudia Barnes giving me knowing looks and asking me *every day*, 'Found out who your dad's shagging yet?' I *so* want to prove Miss

Know-it-All wrong and say, 'You were wrong, Claudia. Dad hasn't got a girlfriend. End of!'

Even Angela Panteli came up to me and said solemnly, 'If you want to talk about anything, just let me know.'

Ange is great, but as I didn't talk to her about anything major *before* Dad left I'm not about to start now, and in any case there really isn't a lot to talk about.

Ideally I would have preferred to use a proper private investigator, as I'm concerned that Freak Boy will think that I owe him something after this, and I'll have to put up with him lurking, sidling up behind me, catching me unawares, whispering, 'What are you going to do for *me*, Electra Brown?' whilst making horrid sucking noises through his teeth.

But then I think of the photograph of Christmas lunch with Dad missing, and the fact that when I'd done a search on the Internet for *private detective* and *rates* I found a Web page which said general investigation was £55 an hour, general surveillance £45 and undercover surveillance up to £150 an hour. I decided I probably needed surveillance rather than investigation, but was stumped as to whether that was general or undercover. Not that it matters. At those rates, for twelve hours, I can't afford a professional private dick anyway. Not unless I cleaned out my building society account, and *then* there'd be questions about what I'd done with the money. I'm sure the parentals would think I'd been buying drugs, or have an online gambling habit or was being blackmailed by someone I'd met through an Internet chat room. Never in a million years would they guess I'd hired a private eye to follow Dad to prove Tits Out doesn't always know *everything* when it comes to men.

I sit in class after class, wondering what Dad is getting up to, and whether he's noticed he's being followed by a creepy beetle on a twenty-four-gear mountain bike.

Chapter Twelve

'Better now, Frazer?' Frosty the Penguin asks in registration the next morning.

FB sits behind me in form class so I can't tell what the expression on his face is. I expect that he nods, because there is silence and then Frosty says, 'Good. Do you have a note from your parents?'

He must have held something up, as she waddles towards me and pauses just behind my desk. There's the sound of an envelope being torn open. I glance over my shoulder to see Frosty's fatty splatty feet are near me and I feel sick. I already feel sick at the thought of what FB might have uncovered.

Two lots of feeling sick don't up add up to feeling twice as sick, more like four times, I think to myself. *Sick squared.*

I momentarily forget to feel ill as I marvel at the fact

that I have actually learnt something in maths after all these years.

'Fine,' says Frosty.

Whilst she waddles back to the front of the class, FB pokes me in the back with what I hope is a ruler. He's sitting too far away for it to be anything else. I put my hand behind me, feel a note, grab it, and then drop it into my lap as if it's a hot Pop-Tart. I feel too scared to open it. This is it. This is the moment I have been both waiting for *and* dreading.

Get a grip, girl! I tell myself, and with sweaty, trembling hands I open the note.

I've written a report on yesterday.

Where shall we meet to discuss it? FB

The bell goes for the first lesson. I am *not* going to be seen to be talking to FB in front of the others, so I make a quick dash for the door. However anxious I am to find out about what Dad is up to, I'm not so desperate that I'll let everyone see that I'm communicating with the beaky alien.

I'm scooting down the corridor towards history when Tits Out calls after me, 'Hey! Electra! Hang on!'

I slow down to a normal walk to let her catch up. Freak Boy isn't going to approach me with Claudia beside me. I can use her and her boobs as a human shield against him.

'Hi, Claudia,' I say, as she approaches, tits first. 'What's up?'

'I hear you're going out with Razor Burns,' she says. 'Since when?'

'Since never!' I gasp. 'Who started that ugly evil rumour?' I narrow my eyes in what I hope is a menacing manner. 'Not *you*, I hope?'

Tits Out doesn't seem affected by my hard stare. I must practise more. Sorrel is a master at shooting withering drop-down-dead looks.

'As if!' says Claudia. 'I *was* surprised when Jags mentioned it. But then I saw Razor pass you a note in reg so I thought it must be true.'

'*You* know *Jags*?' I feel shock, disappointment and jealousy all rolled into one. It's not a nice feeling.

'Well, James, Lucy's brother, really, but as him and Jags hang around together all the time, I know Jags really well too.' She says this in a casual way which suggests that hanging around with The Spanish Lurve God is something she does all the time, the slaggy cow. 'Jags said he'd seen you at Razor's house and then what with the note . . .'

As we go in to the classroom I fling my bag on a

desk and say in my loudest voice, 'I am NOT going out with *anybody*!'

'At least Jags mentioned you,' says Lucy during break. 'I thought you were worried you were a non-person. You can't be invisible if he's talking to Claudia Barnes about you.'

I can't actually see Luce because we're huddled on benches in the science block, hiding under a row of white lab coats, our legs pulled up to our chins, hoping that the sixth-form Nazis who patrol the cloakrooms during break don't spot our legs and order us out. It's brass monkey weather, but another petty Burke's rule means we're forced to stay outside unless it's raining. Obviously the school is concerned we might drown from a torrential downpour, but doesn't care about potential death from hypothermia.

'He wasn't saying *good* things about me. He told Tits Out I was going out with Freak Boy!' I whisper. 'How bad is that?'

'The pits,' admits Lucy. 'Can't you sue him for libel or slander or whatever it is?'

'She knows Jags through *your* brother!' I'm annoyed that being best friends with Lucy seems to have done me no good at all on the Jags front, and that Claudia has pushed herself to the front of the Jags admiration queue, tits first. 'You never said that James knows Tits Out!'

'I don't know what my brother is up to,' says Lucy. 'Do you?'

There's the sound of footsteps in the corridor. We hold our breath, pull our knees up to our ears and wait.

One of the lab coats rustles and a voice whispers, 'Luce? Electra?'

It's Sorrel. There's more rustling as she arranges herself under the lab coats.

'I'm in mega distress,' I hiss.

'About your old man?' asks Sorrel. 'I thought you'd got over that?'

'No, *worse*. There's a rumour going round that I'm going out with FB.'

'That's well gross!' There's pure disgust in her voice. 'Have you snogged him in this rumour?'

'Get lost!' I'm offended she even had such a disgusting thought. FB wouldn't feature on my Snogability Scale as it only deals with humans, and Freak Boy is clearly an alien beetle.

'He's got the results,' I whisper, 'of when he followed Dad. He wants to meet me somewhere, but I can't risk it. If I'm seen, that'll confirm the ugly rumour.'

'Meet him in secret, somewhere that no one else will see you,' suggests Lucy.

'People like Claudia Barnes and her slaggy spies are everywhere,' I say miserably. 'I'm bound to be spotted.'

'I can think of somewhere nobody we know *ever* goes,' says Sorrel. '*I'll* tell Freak Boy where to meet us. No one would dare start a rumour about me and him. I'd kill 'em.'

The bell goes for the third lesson and we emerge, blinking, from beneath the lab coats.

'Brill!' I say. 'Where?'

'Mum's café,' says Sorrel. 'Let's meet him after school at The Bay Tree.'

Chapter Thirteen

In theory it sounds great to have a best friend whose mum runs a café, but in practice it makes no difference. It's not near school or home or anywhere we might want to hang out, plus it's a Face Food-free zone so it doesn't sell meat or milkshakes and Sorrel usually refuses to go there.

The only way Sorrel's mum could afford to rent somewhere was to take a lease on a tiny café in a grotty parade of shops on the outskirts of town. So, wedged in between a shop which sells old fridges and mattresses, and a well-dodgy-looking pub called the Duchess of Kent, is the bright-yellow and green shopfront of The Bay Tree Organic Café.

You wouldn't think that anyone in such a run-down area would be interested in being a lentil, but whenever I've been there are always people coming out clutching brown recycled-paper bags filled with tofu wraps or lentil pâté pittas, sitting at one of the sustainable forest stripped-pine tables nursing a dandelion root coffee, or scanning the hundreds of messages stuck to the noticeboard offering everything from crystal healing to the services of Pawline the pet psychic and paw-reader. I'd like to see *her* try and read Google's paws, though presumably she'd know in advance that the psycho pet would try and savage her fingers.

There was about a week last summer when Lucy and I were in and out of the café because Sorrel was working there. She didn't want to, but her mum was so desperate for holiday staff she *ordered* Sorrel to put on an apron and help out. It all went horribly wrong, because in protest Sorrel started sidling up to customers whispering, 'Would you like a nice bloody steak to go with your alfalfa and chickpea salad?' In the end Yolanda had to sack her own daughter as too many customers were walking out in disgust.

When we arrive, the twins, OJ and BJ, are sitting painting at one of the tables, their cappuccino-coloured hands and faces smeared in brightly coloured poster paint. When they see us they scramble off their chairs and rush over to show us their sticky artwork. Tucked away in a corner near the back of the café, next to the loos, is Senna, bent over what looks like her homework. She could probably have got away with being called after a laxative if she'd been all perky and smiley, but she's porky and sullen with milk-bottle glasses and frizzy black hair, and she barely glances at us.

Sorrel's mum looks up at the commotion.

'Girls! What a lovely surprise!'

She shoots out from behind the counter, shoos the mucky twins away, and makes a beeline for me, giving me a big hug.

'Sorrel told me about your ma and pa. Tell your ma I've been sending her positive energy.' She squeezes me even tighter, so whatever boobs I might have been sprouting have almost certainly been pushed back in. 'It's a bad business. A bad bad business. You doing OK?'

I nod and smile. 'Fine now, thanks.'

I *really* like Yolanda. She's a bit full-on what with always banging on about saving the planet, whales, the curse of Beast Cars, meat is murder and how we'd all be better off being vegan, but with her skinny corkscrew braids cascading over the top of the brightly coloured scarf she always wears wound round her head, and the wide, white smile which lights up her face, whenever I see her, she always makes me feel special.

'To what do I owe this honour?' she asks, finally letting me go as I've begun to gasp for air.

'We're meeting someone about a school project,' says

Sorrel. 'He's got a nose like a beak and he walks like a beetle. You are *not* to be nice to him. We just want some information and then he's going.'

'I am *not* going to be not nice to anyone in *my* café.' Yolanda wags a finger at her daughter. As she turns back to the counter, Sorrel sticks her tongue out. The twins giggle and copy her, and Senna glares at us and hunches further over her books.

We've only just parked our butts on a chair when the door opens and Freak Boy scuttles in clutching a blue plastic folder. He looks nervous and keeps his chin tucked into his neck.

The beetle boy description is so apt, Sorrel's mum instantly knows who he is and calls out, 'Hello, boy! Welcome! My daughter has just been talking about you.'

Sorrel looks daggers at her mum, who doesn't notice as she's too busy pouring apple juice (I *think* it's apple, but it's very cloudy) into green-tinged recycled-glass beakers.

FB sits on one side of the table and the three of us sit on the other, ready to interrogate him. Sorrel's mum brings the beakers – it *is* apple – and when she's gone Sorrel leans forward and hisses, 'Don't get comfy, FB. We just want the information and then we've *finished* with you.'

FB nods, opens the file and pulls out a piece of paper which he slides across the table towards us.

The info is in a table, carefully typed with neat tabs and underlining.

Movements of Mr Rob Brown

1. Proprietor of Plunge It Plumbing Services
2. Father of Electra Brown
3. Possible Adulterer

Aim of Surveillance: To establish if point 3 (above) is correct
Private Investigator: Frazer Burns
Mode of Transport: Mountain bike, 24 gears
Date of Surveillance: Tuesday 23rd January
Additional Notes: Suspect will be hereafter known as RB. Plunge It Plumbing Supplies will hereafter be known as PIPS

Time	Movements & Notes
10.03	RB's van (Ford Transit, blue & white, registration FP55 LFL) parked outside premises of PIPS.
10.42	RB leaves PIPS & drives off in van (details as above). Van moving too fast to catch up but heading in easterly direction.

11.03	Surveillance of area east of PIPS reveals van (details as above) parked outside dental practice of a Mr Lionel Black (BDS, PhD) 22 Aldbourne Road.
13.07	RB leaves 22 Aldbourne Road in van (as above) & heads in westerly direction. Unable to keep up with van. Hunch that RB had returned to PIPS – correct as at:
13.27	RB's van parked outside premises of PIPS.
16.00	RB leaves PIPS premises in van and heads east.
16.15	Investigator passes 22 Aldbourne Road and sees RB trying to park van but failing as road is packed with parents picking up children from King William's School for Boys.
16.17	RB looks annoyed, leans out of van window and gives V-sign to woman double-parked in Range Rover Discovery with hazard lights flashing. (Black, top of the range, registration DTS 624.) RB drives away.
16.21	RB returns to 22 Aldbourne Road on foot & goes inside.
17.30	Investigator leaves the scene.

I read and re-read the report.

'Why did you start at ten?' I ask. 'Where was Dad before ten?'

'I didn't get out of bed before nine-thirty,' Freak Boy admits. 'I was supposed to be ill and I had to be convincing. Mum's a doctor, remember.'

I didn't know FB's mum was a medic. I'm alarmed at the speed with which my imagination makes a rapid leap from Doc FB in a white coat, to Hot Dad in a white coat holding a stethoscope and examining my chest, and have to take a big gulp of chilled apple juice to bring me to my senses.

'And why did you leave him at five-thirty?' Lucy asks. 'What happened after five-thirty?'

Freak Boy looks embarrassed. His shoulders are so hunched his beak is practically touching the table.

'I had to get home before Mum. When she left in the morning she said she'd try and get home early as I was ill.'

Sorrel practically spits her apple juice at him.

'You're bloody useless, FB. This doesn't prove anything!'

'It proves he has a problem with his teeth,' says FB lamely.

'I knew *that*!' I snap. 'He's been having problems with his fangs for ages. Tell me something I don't know.'

Chapter Fourteen

After the Freak Boy fiasco Lucy suggested again that I just popped the trollop question to Dad myself.

'He'd never lie to you,' she said. 'Just ask him outright. If you can't ask him to his face, email him at work.'

So here I am in what used to be the living room but, as we practically live in the kitchen which has a sofa and a television, has now turned into a junk and computer room. There's a sofa bed in here, but I haven't seen the colour of the upholstery for years as there's so much *stuff* on it.

My fingers hover over the keyboard and then I begin typing:

To: *Dad*
From: *SOnotagreekgirl1*
Date: *Thursday 25th January 17.15*

Dad – Hope you're OK and that you haven't been up to your elbows in sewage or, if you have, you've scrubbed the poo from your nails. Ha ha! How are the gnashers? Are they gleaming white but still crumbling?

Anyway, loads of girls at school, especially Sorrel and Claudia, say that you wouldn't have left home if you didn't have some glam totty hanging around behind the scenes. Is that why you left? Do you have some oval-faced, long-limbed, golden-haired modelly girlfriend with high cheekbones and even higher boobs who is a house-proud Cordon Bleu cook who can speak fluent French and does gymnastics?

I stop typing and look back at what I've written. I know I'm being silly. It's just I can't imagine Dad leaving us for someone else, unless this someone else, who may or may not exist, is the complete opposite of Mum and me. A tidy Lurve Goddess who can cook.

I delete the email and start again.

To: Dad
From: SOnotagreekgirl1
Date: Thursday 25th January 17.25

Dad – Hope you're OK and that your teeth aren't giving you too much gyp. Something's been giving ME gyp and I have to ask. Have you left us for someone else?

E xxxx

I decide that I need to be more specific, so after *someone else* I add *Do you have a girlfriend?*

And then I press *Send*.

I sit at the computer for ages, pressing *Refresh* over and over again.

I look at my watch. If Dad's not at the dentist or out at a plumbing job, he'll still be at the office and so should see the email. I'm just about to give up and shut down, when a little yellow envelope pops up.

I open it.

To: SOnotagreekgirl1
From: Dad
Date: 25th January 18.05
Subject: Re: A Question

Hi Electra,
Nice surprise to get your mail.

Of course I haven't got a girlfriend!

See you soon.

Lots of love Dad x

PS Teeth OK thanks. x

Chapter Fifteen

Life is fantastico. Everything is going really well and there's half-term to look forward to next week. Only tomorrow, Thursday and Friday to get through and then the holiday officially starts! Wa-hey!

Me, Luce and Sorrel are still deciding what we're going to do with the week. We've got *loads* of plans. We just need to decide in what order we're going to do them.

I want to spend some time hanging around the sports centre in case The Spanish Lurve God appears. I also want to see if Tits Out is hanging around James to get to Jags. I'll be gutted if she *is* seeing Jags, but on the other hand I'd rather know what I'm dealing with, and if Jags is the sort of boy who finds ant eyebrows, straightened bleached hair and chicken fillet breasts attractive, I don't stand a chance. The plan is to take my camera with me, and if Jags is around I'll pretend I'm taking shots of Luce and Sorrel, whilst really I will be secretly using my zoom to bypass the girls and snap pictures of the lovely Jags looking all sporty and Spanish.

Sorrel wants to go shopping and try on as many pairs of leather shoes and boots as she can in a day. Another downside to the whole vegetarian/vegan scene going on round Sorrel's house is the ban on *any* leather goods. It's not so bad in the summer, but plakky boots in the winter make your feet sweat and pong. Or so Sorrel claims.

Lucy doesn't mind what we do and is happy to come shopping, but isn't bothered about shoes, as her mum has a massive shoe collection and Luce already has the same size feet as Bella. Neat Freak Bella takes a picture of each pair and sticks the snap to the outside of the shoebox so she knows what's inside. Imagine that! Anyway, if we can find a day when Bella is out, Sorrel and I might go round to Lucy's and try on Bella's shoes. It's all designer stuff, and as my trotters are as wide as saucers I can't get much on, but it's fun to watch Sorrel practically hyperventilate as each box is opened and the smell of expensive leather hits her nose. Once, for a laugh, Sorrel and I put the wrong shoes back in the wrong boxes *on purpose*, but Luce got into so much trouble we felt *terrible*, so now we're para about making sure everything gets put away carefully, and hardly ever go to Lucy's.

At some point Jack, Mum and me are going to see Nana Pat for tea. As Dad is living there I might suggest to him that he takes an afternoon off which will please Nana. Although we usually see her quite a bit as she doesn't live far, we haven't seen her since before Christmas and she rarely sees us all together, what with Dad working all the time.

The rest of the week we'll fill up with lolling about in my bedroom reading magazines, re-evaluating the S-Scale and generally trying to forget about school for a week. We won't go to Sorrel's. We *never* hang out at Sorrel's. She hates sharing a bedroom with Snitchy Jasmine, Senna is like an evil energy-sapping force when she's in the house, even if she's not in the room, and the twins are always hanging around with snotty noses wanting us to play with them. Sunday night will be spent trying to finish all the home-work that's due in on Monday. If I don't get it finished, I'll hijack one of the Geeks who sit at the front of the bus on Monday morning and get them to give me the answers.

Bang in the middle of half-term is Valentine's Day. The postman will *not* be staggering towards the door of 14 Mortimer Road, his back breaking with the weight of Valentine's cards destined for me, as every year for as long as I can remember the *only* card I *ever* get is from Dad. He gets someone at the office to write the envelope so I won't recognize his writing, but I always know it's from him as I recognize the way he does an X for a kiss, sort of small and tight and spidery. Lucy will, as usual, get masses. Last year it was a record six. We always have great fun trying to decipher the writing and working out who they might be from. Last year, Paul Cottismore really cocked things up by addressing the card to *Miss Malone* and then signing it *Regards, P Cottismore*. Loser! I *so* wanted to post it on a noticeboard at school so everyone could have a laugh at *Regards, P Cottismore's* expense, but Luce wouldn't let me, even though she said she'd rather stick hot pins in her eyes than go out with him. Sorrel has always claimed that if she ever got a card and found out who sent it, she'd ram it up their backside, complete with envelope and stamp, so it's not surprising her Valentine card count is always zero.

As I'm lying on my bed thinking of lurved-up things, an image of Tits Out and Jags pops into my head. They're laughing and holding hands and running through a field of golden corn. *I* want to be in that cornfield with Jags, but obviously without Claudia poking her tits out. There must be *some* way I can get closer to him.

I've considered pretending my hip joint is about to collapse so that I can get an appointment with Dr Garcia at the hospital, but the thought of being prodded and poked and X-rayed and scanned with no guarantee that Jags would even come up in the conversation is too much of a risk, or worse, that he might pop in to see his dad and catch me wearing one of those hideous green surgical gowns which don't do up at the back and see my bum sticking out.

Another possibility I've considered is to adopt a Spanish theme in the way I dress. I've abandoned my initial idea of only wearing the colours of the Spanish flag, as the blood-and-pus colour scheme isn't really me, what with being pasty and pale rather than olive-skinned and exotic. Mum still has a flamenco doll, a cheesy reminder of where she and Dad met, but although in that get-up he's bound to notice me, I might feel a bit odd in a huge ruffled skirt, fan and big headdress, hanging about the sports centre.

I just don't know what to do. The mags all bang on about showing a boy your sparkling personality as well as your bits, but if Jags barely looks at me and never speaks to me, how can my personality even glimmer let alone sparkle?

I've been over the Compton Avenue incident again and again. Not only was I dressed as a tramp, I was tongue-tied too. I'm such a slug-head I didn't even know Jags was quoting Shakespeare when he was going on about protesting too much.

That's it! I think. Billy Boy Shakespeare can come to my rescue! I'll learn a couple of quotes which I can casually toss into the conversation should I see Jags during the *hours* I'm hanging around the sports centre, holding a badminton racket I never intend to use, hoping to accidentally-on-purpose bump into him. I'm not quite sure what I'd do if he actually challenged me to a game of badminton as my hand–eye coordination is dismal. I don't think I could handle a speeding shuttlecock even for The Spanish Lurve God.

I go downstairs to the computer.

Jack is playing Worms Armageddon.

'Get off,' I say. 'I need to do homework.'

'Can't,' says Jack. 'I've just used a sheep launcher and I want a skunk.'

'Get off!' I try and wrestle his hand away from the keyboard as a worm shrieks, 'You idiot!'

Jack hunches protectively over the keyboard and the sound of weapons exploding and worms speaking fills the room.

'Want Mum to know you're a bicycle-lamp-thieving runt?' I hiss in his ear.

He jumps away from the keyboard as if he's been electrocuted and runs out of the room.

Works every time.

I've done a search for famous Shakespeare quotes which has thrown up literally millions of websites.

I pick the first one.

It seems to me that James and Jags have already used the best quote. I can't imagine meeting Jags outside the sports centre and casually slipping, 'Do you think I am easier to be played on than a pipe?' into the conversation. He might run a mile if I say, 'This is the very ecstasy of love.'

After more searching I decide that *I like this place and willingly could waste my time in it*, from *As You Like It*, would be useful if he sees me outside the sports centre, and *Nothing will come of nothing* from *King Lear* is good, mostly because it's short and I'm bound to remember it.

I'm still scanning the list of Billy's plays when there's a key in the lock, the front door opens and Dad comes in. He puts his head round the living-room door and says, 'I'm just popping in to check the timer on the boiler is working. Your mum said the central heating was coming on at odd times.'

Dad is still always popping in and out to do things. Fiddling with Mum's car. Changing a light fitting. Putting a new washer on a tap in the bathroom. Actually, I don't know why he bothered to say he was moving out in the first place. Nothing much seems to have changed. He was always either at work, on the way to work, just in from work but probably going out again, so that his 'popping in and out', as he puts it, seems entirely normal. Sometimes I don't even bother to look up from the telly when he comes in. He sort of hovers by the sofa as if he expects me to say something, or throw my arms around him and gush, 'Hi, Dad!' but as I never did that in the first place, I'm definitely not going to start now. In fact life is so normal it seems to me that Mum and Dad could have pretended things were OK for ever and ever and I would never have noticed they weren't.

I hear Mum and Dad talking downstairs in the kitchen. Dad's laughing at something Mum must have said.

Some kids make such a fuss when their parents separate, I think. They bang on about being from a broken home, how there are always arguments when their parents meet, or battles over visiting rights, writing to mag problem pages to whine on about how crap their life has become. What a bunch of pathetic lame-o's! They should get a life and stop moaning. There's no need for it. We're a model for other separated families to follow. Jack is fine now I've thwarted his career as a petty criminal. Mum is fine, in fact she's looking *really* good now she's lost some weight and is doing the Fern stuff. Google is fine and enjoying the extra cabbage leaves, though I don't think he's fine enough for me to actually get him out of the cage without losing a fingertip. Dad seems *very* relaxed. I can't imagine him getting all stressy-headed over a peach stone now. Mum was right. He just needed some space and a breather to get over the whole ageing coot-head scene. He'll be popping back in with his cases any day now and no one will say anything. It will be as if the Big Announcement had never happened.

It's all very well Sorrel being all sniffy and chippy about the fact that we're a family of clams, but if we'd made a big fuss, you know, sat down and talked about things and made an issue out of Dad needing some space to himself, he'd *never* come back. Dad has just quietly had his mid-life crisis and got over it.

I look down the list of plays Billy Boy penned.

Parents separating, I think, *is Much Ado about Nothing.*

Chapter Sixteen

Thursday evening. Only tomorrow to get through and then at ten to four half-term officially begins. I can't *wait* to pull off my foul school tie and not put it on again for over a week. Even though I keep the knot as large and low and loose as possible, sometimes it feels like a green polyester noose around my neck.

I'm sitting at the kitchen table, head bent, going cross-eyed staring at my hair, trying to snip off split ends with a pair of nail scissors.

Jack is doing something in his room, or on the computer.

Mum is chopping cabbage into huge chunks for her cabbage soup.

I'm *amazed* that she's managed to stick to the diet and do Fern's exercises. I really thought that after a couple of days she'd give up and go back to chocolate, the sofa and Sudoku. She's had her hair cut – shoulder length with a flick up at the end – and it's now officially Burnt Chestnut rather than mousy brown with the odd bit of grey.

Mum is *definitely* looking good.

Even the girls have noticed a difference. They came back after school today. We're still working our way through Jack's football magazine and assigning Snogability Scores. It's been difficult because in the official team shots some players look hot, but then when they're photographed running for the ball or doing other footballery-type things they pull weird faces as if they're having a seizure, and this rather puts us off. One shot showed a previously 4S player spitting and blowing snot out of his nose at the same time, so his score immediately plummeted to 2.7S and would have been a 1.5S had he not been a footballer. Snogs and snot are not a happy combination, noses and mouths being in such close proximity to each other. Also, anyone with a Spanish-sounding name gets an extra point in honour of Jags. It's my room, my mag (well, Jack's) and so my rules.

When Lucy saw Mum, she said, 'You look *fantastic*, Mrs B!'

'Foxy mum!' Sorrel added, giving a rare smile which made her look the spitting image of her mum.

Mum blushed and laughed off the compliment, but it was obvious she was chuffed.

The *moment* we got up into my room Sorrel whispered, 'Do you think your mum has tarted herself up to get your old man back?'

I gave Sorrel a *Who knows?*-type of look, because of *course* it had crossed my mind, but I didn't need Sorrel to point it out, and anyway Mum's glam plan to get Dad home seems to be working.

'What day are we going to Nana Pat's for tea?' I ask Mum.

'I must ring her,' she says, starting to hack at another green orb. 'It's strange that she hasn't been on the phone. I haven't spoken to her since we rang her at Uncle Richard's on Christmas Day.'

'I need to know because I can't make defo plans until I do,' I say, aware that a slight whingey note is coming into my voice. 'It's such a pain.'

As if on cue, the phone rings.

'That's probably her now, or someone trying to sell me a kitchen. Can you get it, love?' Mum asks.

I get up from the table and go to pick up the phone. 'Hello?'

'I need to speak to a Mrs Brown.' It's a clipped, stern, male voice.

'Who is it calling?'

'Potter,' the man says. 'Mr Potter. I'm the store manager at Tesco Extra at Eastwood Circle.'

'Hang on, please.'

I hold the phone out to Mum.

'Some guy from the big Tesco's wants to speak to you.'

Mum looks puzzled, but wipes her cabbage hands on a tea towel and takes the phone.

'This is Mrs Brown speaking.'

I sit back down at the table, grab another handful of hair and start searching for split ends to destroy. They're rampant. I should never have let my hair get so long without at least a trim. I trim my fringe all the time so that it's always just the right length, not dorky short, and not so long I have to keep blowing upwards to keep it out of my eyes. I can't believe that in an attempt to make my face look longer I've let the ends of my hair get so rank. If I'm not careful, the split ends will run all the way up so I'll *have* to get my hair cut. Then the hairdresser will say, 'You'll need about two inches off,' which of course means four, as hairdressers have a very weird sense of what is an inch and never use metric, and I'll then find I've got hair at chin length, my face will look *massive* and I'll have to go out after dark like a vampire. Plus, I *hate* going to the hairdresser's as you're forced to look at yourself in the mirror, and the wide-face, wet-hair and bright-lights combo is especially minging.

I'm not really listening to Mum on the phone, I'm still snipping split ends and then sweeping them from the table on to the floor with my hand, but I hear Mum say, 'I can assure you that you've got the wrong Jack Brown. It's a very common name. My Jack is upstairs in his room.'

There must be more talking at the other end, because Mum puts her hand over the receiver and says, 'Electra love, run upstairs and get Jack, will you?' She makes frantic nodding movements towards the door with her head in a way which suggests I need to get off my backside and get upstairs quickly.

'My daughter is just getting him. We won't keep you.'

I shoot upstairs. There's no sound of worms being massacred from the living room, but I pop my head round the door to be sure. No sign of Jack, just clutter and the computer. I'm about to shoot up to his room when I feel a blast of cold air and I notice that the front door is half open. A bad sign, but not one hundred per cent proof of desertion. I take the stairs two at a time and put my head round his bedroom door. Smelly and empty. From the basement I can hear Mum shouting up, 'Electra! Have you found him?'

'He's gone!' I yell down, hanging over the banister.

By the time I get back downstairs Mum is already at the door with her coat on.

'What's happened?' I ask.

'Ring your dad. Tell him to meet me at the big Tesco's at Eastwood. He should ask for the store manager, a Mr Potter.'

'What's going on?' I ask again.

'Electra, for heaven's sake just do it!' Mum orders, scrabbling around in her bag for her car keys.

'Mum?' I practically yell.

Mum finds her keys, which are on the floor under the side table, and heads out of the front door into the night.

'Jack's been caught shoplifting,' she shouts over her shoulder.

I use the house phone to try Dad's moby.

It switches straight to voicemail.

Hello, this is Rob Brown. I'm sorry I'm not here to take your call, but please leave your name . . .

I cancel the call. That's odd. Dad *always* answers his phone or leaves it switched on.

I try the office in case he's working late.

The offices of Plunge It Plumbing Services are now shut. For out-of-hours plumbing emergencies, please ring our twenty-four-hour number . . .

I put the phone down.

Nana Pat. Dad's living with Nana Pat.

I rifle through the address book, find her number and dial it.

'Pat Brown.'

'Nana! It's Electra!'

I swear I can hear a sharp intake of breath at the other end of the line before she says, 'How are you darlin'?'

'Fine, fine.' I'm impatient. 'Look, is Dad back from work yet? I need to speak to him urgently.'

'Is everything all right?' Nana sounds concerned. 'Someone taken sick?'

'No, no one, but I need to speak to Dad. It's important.'

'He's not 'ere, darlin', but I can get a message to 'im,' she says and rings off.

I don't know what to do next and start pacing the floor. I'm sure she won't be able to contact him. If *I* can't get through to his office or his mobile, what's *she* going to do? I decide to try his moby again and leave a message for him to call home urgently. I'm just about to ring him when the house phone goes. It's Dad. I gabble about Jack and Tesco's and tell him to meet Mum at the store.

'Bloody hell!' he snaps, and the phone clicks off.

As I put the receiver down, something is niggling me.

How come Nana Pat could get a message to him and I couldn't?

I pick up the phone again and dial 1471. A prim female staccato voice recites the number of the last call. 'Dial 3 to return the call,' orders Prim Voice.

I press 3.

There's the sound of electronic dialling, a few rings and then a woman answers. 'Hello?'

I freeze.

'Hello? Hello?' the voice repeats like a demented parrot.

And then I unfreeze and slam the phone down.

I hear the low heavy vibration of a van pulling up outside. Then a car and the sound of several sets of doors slamming. I glance at my watch. Seven-thirty. About an hour has passed since Mum left. I've just been sitting here at the table, mostly staring into space, dealing with the randomly stupid questions which popped into my mind, such as *How long does an ant live?* and *Why do you never see any baby pigeons?* but occasionally snipping the odd split end, no longer in the mood for serious trimming. I know that Jack will be in *big* trouble and, much as my little bro annoys me and I want to know what's gone on, I don't really want to see him given the third degree by the parentals. But before I can get up from the table, there's the sound of a key in the front door and Mum ordering, 'Go to your room.'

I hear Jack scampering up the stairs and slamming his bedroom door, so I decide to stay put.

Mum and Dad come down to the kitchen. They both look absolutely drained. Mum still has her coat on and goes over to click on the kettle. She then opens the fridge and offers Dad a can of beer.

'I'm driving, remember?' he snaps at her.

'What happened?' I ask them.

'Jack was caught shoplifting,' sighs Mum, putting the beer back in the fridge.

Dad says nothing but has a grim look on his face.

'He was spotted on the security video stuffing a box of forty Super Plus Tampax under his anorak,' Mum says. 'They'd been watching him as they thought it was odd that an eight-year-old boy was interested in that aisle.'

I am *furious*. If you're going to shoplift, and I am *not* suggesting anyone should, then at least nick something useful. What was Jack going to do with forty tampons? Draw faces on them and play soldiers?

'He *promised* me he wouldn't do it again,' I explode, realizing too late that I'd said the wrong thing at the wrong time to the wrong people.

Dad's face darkens. 'What do you mean, *again*?'

I gulp. I've gone too far to pull back. There's no point in saying anything other than, 'I found out he was stealing lights from bikes outside the sports centre.'

Most of the time I try and pretend that Jack's not around, or that The Little Runt is someone else's annoying brother, but I feel upset that I've squealed on him. I feel as if I've crossed to the other side, the dark side, the land of the parentals and their weird ways. By snitching on him I'm no longer one of us, but one them. Judas!

'Jeez, Ellie,' Dad shouts. 'I've only been gone just over five weeks and already my son is on his way to getting a criminal record. What the hell has been going on round here?'

'Don't exaggerate, Rob,' Mum says, taking off her coat. She looks good with the new haircut and lost weight, but Dad is too furious to notice. He's pacing the kitchen floor.

'You heard that store manager guy,' he yells. 'He wanted to know why a lad his age was out in the evening, wandering around in the dark on his own!'

Mum starts to look angry. Now she's lost a bit of weight and the double chin is less double, more sort of one and two-thirds of one, I can see her jaw is clenched.

'I've told you,' she says stiffly. 'I thought he was upstairs. We *both* did.'

She glances at me as if she needs support, and so I nod enthusiastically.

Dad stomps around the kitchen table, pausing to bang his fist on it. I begin to feel a bit scared. This feels even more nuclear than the Curious Incident of the Peach Stone on the Kitchen Floor. 'What were the two of you doing whilst Jack was gallivanting around planning to rob shops? Sitting on the sofa stuffing your faces with chocolate?'

Mum looks as if she might explode, and I'm *furious* with Dad for dragging me into this. If your little brother decides to creep out of the house before tea, get on a bus to a shopping centre and go into a supermarket to nick feminine protection, it seems to me there isn't much you can do about it.

'It's just attention seeking,' says Mum. 'It'll be a phase, like when he thought it was funny to say *fart* all the time.'

'And why does he feel the need to seek attention?' snaps Dad. 'Have you asked yourself that?'

I'm about to say, *Perhaps because you left home*, but before I can open my mouth I notice Mum and Dad looking past me. Jack has appeared in the kitchen. Everyone has been so busy arguing we hadn't heard him come down the stairs. His face is red and swollen from crying. He's carrying a Tesco plastic bag in one hand and his football in the other.

'I don't want to live here any more,' he says, sobbing. 'I want to go and live with Dad at Nana Pat's. I've packed my football boots and shirt.'

He holds out the plastic bag and I think my heart will break, but only for a moment, when I realize that if he lived at Nana Pat's it would mean he wouldn't be able to hog the computer playing Worms. Now that I've used my trump card by telling the parentals about the bike lights, it's going to be harder to get him off without severe physical violence. I can't *wait* for my birthday when I've been promised my own laptop.

Dad goes over and crouches down in front of Jack. 'That's not possible, son,' he says softly. 'You live here, with Mum and Electra and Google. You'd have to change schools and you'd miss your friends.'

'But I don't have any friends now Freddie's moved. I want to stay with you and Nana,' he wails. 'If you won't let me, I'll just run away and turn up at her door. I know how to get there.'

Dad stands up. His face has a strange, twisted look.

'Look, Rob, how about it?' Mum says. 'It's half-term next week. He could spend the week with you and come back at the weekend.'

Jack starts jumping up and down with delight. 'Yeah! Yeah! Can I bring my table football? Can we go and

157

see Arsenal play? Can I eat Pot Noodles *every* day?'

I'm pleased too. The thought of a whole week having the remote control to myself, not having to wrestle Jack off the computer or puncture my feet by stepping on a stray stegosaurus is *very* appealing.

'It's not as simple as that.' Dad's voice is wobbly. He glances at Mum, then looks across at me, back to Jack and then to Mum again. His eyes seem to be ping-ponging around the room. For a moment I wonder if he's on drugs, his pupils seem so dilated.

'Pat will be delighted to keep an eye on him when you're out at work,' says Mum. 'What's the problem?'

Dad starts swallowing madly. I can see the Adam's apple in his throat bobbing up and down. I think of the woman answering the number I dialled and begin to feel a sense of gut-wrenching rising panic. Dad orders Jack and me to leave the room, but only Jack scampers off. I have a *very* bad feeling about this, but I *have* to stay. It's like when you pass an accident. You know you shouldn't gawp, but you can't help but peer at the person lying on the road all bashed up, blood spilling on the tarmac.

I push back my chair and pull my knees up to my chin. 'I'm staying,' I say defiantly.

Dad gives me an odd look, but I don't move. His eyes

are still boomeranging around, his Adam's apple is bobbing and beads of sweat dot his forehead.

'Um . . . the thing is, Ellie . . . there's no easy way of saying this . . . I didn't want you to find out like this . . . the thing is, well, to tell you the truth I'm not actually living at my mother's. Haven't been for a while. Not since I left.'

I wish I'd done as Dad asked and left the room. It's too late now. I feel paralysed, stuck to the chair with fear. I can't look at Mum. I can't look at Dad. There's so much tension in the air I feel as if I can hardly breathe. All I can do is hold on to my knees.

'Where are you living?' Mum's voice doesn't sound upset, or angry. It's just slow and flat.

'Well, I wasn't being entirely honest when I said I just needed time and space. I mean, I *did* need time away, I needed to be sure, before I told you, you know, um, that I was doing the right thing, because I needed to be really sure, there was no point in telling you if it wasn't going to work out . . .'

Dad is babbling.

From somewhere I find the courage to glance up.

Mum is standing at the kitchen units. Beside her is a pile of cabbage chunks, a knife and the cabbage she'd abandoned when the phone rang. She puts her hand on the knife and says in the same slow, flat voice, 'What are you trying to say?'

I notice Dad glance at the knife, and he backs towards the kitchen door.

'That I'm living with someone. She's called Candy. She's a dental hygienist.'

I feel as if I've been punched in the stomach. I'm glad I've got my knees to hug or I might faint and topple off the chair. This feels worse than seeing any knocked-down cyclist or mangled car with blood on the windows. I feel as if I'm in some sort of slow-motion collision between Mum and Dad.

There's an unbearable silence before Mum asks, 'How long has it been going on?' Her grip tightens around the knife. When Dad doesn't answer immediately she growls, 'I said, how *long*?'

'A couple of months, maybe a bit longer, I don't know . . .'

There's another never-ending silence, and then Mum lets out a single, terrible wounded moan. 'Nooooooo!'

'Ellie, I'm so sorry.' Dad looks pathetic standing in the kitchen doorway. For the first time he looks as if he no longer belongs in our kitchen, our house, our family.

He turns to face me. 'Electra, this isn't about you or Jack . . .'

'Get out!' Mum yells.

'Ellie . . .'

'Get out!'

'I can't just go like—'

'GET OUT!'

Mum drops the knife. She picks up chunks of cabbage and begins to throw them at Dad but aims too high so they hit the ceiling above his head, exploding into ribbons of pale green which shower down on his balding head like a vegetable firework.

'GET OUT, ROB BROWN,' she screams. 'GET OUT OR I SWEAR TO GOD I'LL KILL YOU.'

Chapter Seventeen

It's just gone ten-thirty.

I'm sitting on the landing. I've been sitting here for hours.

To my left I can hear Jack still sobbing in his room.

To my right I can hear Mum pacing the floor in hers, clattering around, full of hurt and fury.

They disappeared into their rooms shortly after Dad walked out of the front door brushing cabbage shreds from his shoulders.

I sat on the bottom stair and watched him leave. Behind me, on the landing at the top of the stairs sat Jack, crying, clutching his football and *pleading* with Dad not to go, saying he was sorry he'd stolen things and would never do it again if Dad stayed. He'd obviously been listening to the row all along. Mum stayed in the kitchen. I could hear her screaming, stabbing the hell out of the remains of the cabbage.

Before he left Dad paused at the door, looked down at me and then up at Jack and choked out, 'I'm so sorry.'

I didn't speak to him. I *couldn't* speak. I couldn't cry. Still can't. I think my tear ducts have shut down with shock. I can feel pressure in my head and around the bridge of my nose as if I'm going to cry, but my eyes are bone dry.

As I heard his van drive away all I could think was *All this time Dad has been lying to us through his newly whitened teeth.*

I feel stunned. Sure, the Big Announcement had thrown me for a few days, but after the initial shock, because Dad was always popping in and out and he'd emailed that he hadn't got a girlfriend, I hadn't really taken him leaving seriously. I'd felt sure he was coming back. We'd given him space, we'd given him time. He'd given us lies. There was no mid-life crisis, just some home-wrecking trollopy bitch called Candy. All this time he'd been enjoying the best of both worlds. The cosy family *and* her. He'd been hedging his bets, lying to us until he'd decided whether *she* was better than us. And, it turns out, she is.

After he'd gone and Mum and Jack had rushed into their rooms and slammed their doors, I started to go to my room but sort of got stuck here on the landing, worried about Jack and Mum, not wanting to leave them to go to the top the house. One of the things I love about my bedroom is that being in the roof it feels separate from the family, my own space away from everyone else, but tonight I want to be around them, even if they are on the other side of closed doors, devastated. I did go in to see Mum. She was lying curled up on the bed like a baby, sobbing, banging the mattress with a clenched fist. When she saw me she screamed at me to get out. When I peered round Jack's door he was under his duvet, crying.

My body aches with sitting in one place for so long, so I get up and trudge downstairs to the kitchen, picking my way through the cabbage debris.

I pick up my moby which I'd left on the kitchen table, flop down on the sofa and compose a text to Lucy and Sorrel. My fingers feel stiff with tension as I jab the keys.

`Dad has gf Mum launched cabbage missile attack on enemy Bad scene here Gone 4 good`

I set the phone to vibrate so as not to disturb the others, press *Send* and clutch it.

Within moments it's dancing in my hand.

Lucy.

'Do you want me to come round? Or do you want to come here?' She's crying for me.

'Thanks, but they need me here.'

'Just ring, any time, even if it's like two in the morning.'

I feel the moby vibrate once and glance at the screen.

'I've got a text from Sorrel,' I say. 'I'll see you tomorrow. Look, thanks, Luce.'

'Zillions of cyber hugs. And remember, ring anytime. Love you.'

I press *Open*.

Sorrel's text says, Told u so

Chapter Eighteen

I've gone to school today, even though I've hardly slept. Until I went to get into bed I hadn't realized that I was still wearing my school uniform, but by then I was too knackered to take it off, plus by the time I'd cleared up the cabbage ammunition from the kitchen it was *very* late.

I can confirm that sleeping in your uniform does considerably save time in the morning, but the downside is you feel like a piece of crumpled smelly rubbish. On the other hand, it might be worth doing again, but on a night when my parents haven't had a blazing row over Dad running off with his mistress, and I've had more than two hours' sleep. If I'd slept in my shoes I could have saved another ten to fifteen seconds, but even I think that's gross.

I wanted to stay at home to be with Mum, but she insisted I went to school, even though I don't think missing the last day before half-term would matter. She looks weird. Zombie Mum. Dazed and vacant as if someone has sucked the personality out of her. She just went through the motions of getting breakfast for Jack and organizing his school bag, hardly saying a word. She didn't even notice the kitchen was spotless as I'd cleaned it and sprayed lots of air freshener around to get rid of cabbage pong.

The bus was empty of Burke's kids as I'd missed the usual one, and since Mum was taking Jack to school I couldn't get a last-minute lift. This year he's been allowed to walk by himself as Hilmartin Junior School is only a couple of streets away, but after yesterday's Tesco incident Mum's obviously not taking any chances in case he works his way through all the supermarkets, and comes home with more Tampax and a bumper pack of panty liners.

As I was so late the gates were already closed, so I had to be buzzed in and sign the late register at the school secretary's office.

'Reason for being late?' Mrs Jones asks, her pen poised.

'Some trollopy bitch,' I say bitterly.

Lucy's been completely gorge about the whole thing. She gave me a big hug when we had first break and frogmarched me to the tuck stall to buy me a Twix *and* a Flake. She's asked just the right sort of questions, such as *Is there anything I can do?* and *How are you feeling?* without demanding all the sordid details.

And Sorrel? I feel *terrible* even thinking this as Sorrel is a bezzie, but she's been a major disappointment on the sympathy front. She *says* she's sorry about how things have turned out, but I can't help feeling she's a bit half-hearted about it, and there's a triumphant feeling about her, like she's pleased she's been proved right. That's the sort of attitude I expect from Tits Out, not Sorrel. I could be wrong and I'm *very* tired, and I'm also worried that my white shirt is a bit stinky what with wearing it for three days (it wasn't clean yesterday) *and* sleeping in it. I think Luce thinks I'm trying not to cry, as she keeps flashing me sympathetic *Be brave* looks, but really I'm leaning over the desk and burying my head to sniff my armpits, not to have a secret sob.

Anyway, I've made it through to French, but I'm feeling pretty crappola.

We're streamed in French. I'm in the bottom set, Sorrel is in the top one and Lucy's in the middle but claims she's hurtling towards my lot. She used to be OK, but then Bella started forcing Luce to speak French at home one evening a week as well as extra tuition after school, so now Luce feels Frogged-out and hates it as much as I do.

I'm sure that I'm naturally rubbish at languages, but it doesn't help that we bottom-set dwellers have the world's worst French teacher, a teacher who speaks French with a Geordie accent.

When Mademoiselle Armstrong starts a lesson, instead of the beautiful melodic tones of 'Bonjour la classe,' it sounds more like 'Bon-jew-er laa kal-las,' as she sing-songs her way through the greeting. I may not be any good at French, but even I know that doesn't sound right.

Armstrong is an apt name for her. She looks as if she could wrestle an Olympic shot-putter to the ground with just her little finger, without even breaking a sweat. There's also a rumour that she might have a touch of the lesbionics, as she lives with Miss North, the games teacher, who looked at my thighs long enough to come to the sturdy conclusion and has a rainbow sticker in the back of her car.

I'm sitting in the language lab, half hearing the Big Geordie drone on, and sort of noticing her pointing at the whiteboard, when suddenly I feel my heart clattering away in my chest and I feel dizzy. I try to tell myself that it's just because I'm tired and am having a chocolate-induced blood sugar rush, but the clattering heart and dizziness won't go away. Then my stomach goes into a knot and I begin to feel sweaty. The fluorescent lights seem twice as bright and the walls of the classroom feel as if they're closing in and are going to crush me.

'*Fais attention!*' the Big G yells in my direction. '*Qu'y a-t-il?*'

I can't even pretend that I don't understand what she's saying because I'm feeling ill. I wouldn't know at the best of times.

Mademoiselle Armstrong repeats her question more slowly as if I'm a total slug-head.

'I think I'm going to be sick,' I say to her.

'*En français!*' she orders. '*En français!*'

I can't think what to say, but I know I have to get out of her class quickly if I'm not to barf all over the desk, so I say the first French thing that comes into my head, '*Je voudrais to vomit,*' before legging it out of the language lab and towards the cloakrooms with my hand over my mouth.

I feel better after I've been sick, even though the smell of bleach in the toilets is overpowering and as I was bent over the white porcelain I noticed disgusting brown splatters just under the rim.

170

I look at myself in the mirror. School loo mirrors are *especially* evil. They make the gorgeous-looking girls look even more gorge, and the mingers mega minging. My face looks even wider than ever, more full-sized satellite rather than mini-dish. I splash some water on my face. On TV when people do that they instantly look perky and refreshed. When I look up from the basin I've just got a large pale wet face with a dripping fringe and black mascara circling my eyes. The spotty Goth look has never suited me.

The door opens and Angela Panteli comes in carrying my bag. It's weird that she's in bottom French, what with her being able to speak fluent English *and* Greek. I sort of assume if you can learn one language you can learn any.

'Did the Big G tell you to hunt me down?' I ask.

Ange hands me my bag. 'She said someone should go after you and I volunteered. Oh, and she's told me to tell you that the verb to vomit is *vomir*.'

'Thanks,' I say, leaning against a basin and dabbing my damp face with a scratchy blue paper towel. I feel I owe Ange an explanation as to why I've chucked up in case she thinks I'm one of the bingeing barfing bulimics who regularly hug the toilet bowl. 'I feel a bit trashed 'cause I didn't sleep much last night. I found out my dad's living

171

with some trollop called . . . Candy.' I can hardly bring myself to say her name, especially as it's one of my most hated ones. I also think it's very inappropriate that someone involved in tooth hygiene should have a name connected with confectionery.

'I know,' says Angela softly, touching me on the arm. 'I'm *so* sorry.'

For a moment I think that Lucy or Sorrel must have told someone like Tits Out who has then broadcast it round the school, but neither of them would ever do that. Freak Boy might have heard us talking if he'd been lurking without us knowing, but he wouldn't dare interact with the exotic Angela.

'You do?' I gasp. 'How come?'

Angela looks genuinely concerned, and although I'm feeling grotty I can't help but notice what dark eyes and long eyelashes she has, and feel a millisecond of jealousy. Our names are the wrong way round. With her exotic looks she'd be much better off as an Electra, whereas I'm more of your average Angela.

'I've seen them together,' she says. 'When I've been helping out in the restaurant.'

'And you never told me?'

'Dad says what starts in the restaurant stays in the restaurant. People think that as it's all dark corners and candles they're not going to be spotted, but I know *lots* of things about *lots* of people.'

She doesn't say this in a boasting Tits Out sort of way, she says it in a heavy sad way, as if she knows *loads* of goss which she'd rather she didn't. I have visions of all these couples, none of them married to each other, sitting in The Galloping Greek devouring the mixed meze and souvlaki, discussing how much better their lives would be if they left their families. It makes me so angry I want to storm the restaurant, tie them to their chairs and force-feed them aubergine purée as punishment.

'What does she look like?' I hate myself for being curious, but I have to know. 'Is she a tart?'

'She's just ordinary,' says Angela, shrugging. '*Very* ordinary.'

I'm *horrified*. If Dad was going to run off he might have run off with a bit of arm candy, a trophy girlfriend with Barbie-doll proportions, not some bog-standard ordinary woman.

My moby vibrates and I look into my bag. The screen is flashing *Dad*.

'It's Deceitful Dad,' I say, getting the phone out and holding it as if it's infected with some deadly flesh-eating virus.

'Go on, answer it,' Angela urges, and disappears.

I go in to a cubicle, sit on a closed toilet seat and press *Answer*.

'Yes?' I don't even need to try to sound pissed off with Dad. I am.

'Oh!' He sounds surprised to hear me. 'I didn't expect you to answer. I thought you'd be in lessons.'

'Then why are you ringing?'

'I was going to leave you a message.'

Anything rather than speak to me, I think. *Coward.*

'So, tell me what you were going to say.'

There's silence.

'Go on,' I urge. 'Say whatever it was you were going to say when you knew I couldn't answer back. Pretend I'm the answerphone.' I put on my most sneery sarky voice. 'Please leave your message after the beep. Beeeep!'

I can hear Dad clear his throat.

'I was just going to say that your mum and me splitting up is nothing to do with Jack and you. I still love you. We both do. Your mum and me are not going to be together any more but we can still do things together, as a family . . .'

'Yeah, right!' I spit down the phone.

'Don't be like that!'

'You lied! You said you didn't have anyone and you did!'

'Sometimes grown-ups have to do these things. When you're older and you eventually get a boyfriend you'll—'

I cut him off before he can embarrass himself, and me, any more.

'Don't patronize me with your *you're too young to understand* crap,' I snap. 'Dress it up all you want. The fact of the matter is you haven't just left Mum, you've left *all* of us. Some Bitch Troll with a stupid name is worth more to you than your family.'

'Candy is *not* a bitch!' Dad snaps back. 'And it's short for Candice.'

I am *nuclear* furious that he has defended The Bitch Troll. He makes things even worse by adding, 'You'll like her in time, I know you will.'

I'm so angry my head begins to pound. I feel dizzy and sick again. I stand up and get the toilet seat open just in time. As I've already flushed away the contents of my stomach, there's nothing left to bring up, so all I do is retch and fill my mouth with frothy burning acid. The vomity taste reminds me of aubergines which sets me off retching again. I can hear Dad on the other end of the phone shouting, 'Electra! Electra! Are you OK?'

After a few more dry heaves I feel a bit better, wipe my mouth on the sleeve of my blazer and hiss down the phone, 'Let's get one thing straight. Never in a million, billion, trillion, zillion years will I *ever* like The Bitch Troll.'

And then I retch, again and again.

Chapter Nineteen

World War Three has broken out, and the headquarters of military operations are based at 14 Mortimer Road, specifically in our basement kitchen. Deceitful Dad is enemy number one, closely followed by Nana Pat, who is charged with the war crime of shielding the enemy. All members of the species *Dentata hygienicus* are included, just because if you've been betrayed by one, they're all tarred with the same toothbrush.

The first attack on the enemy became clear when the Big G sent me home early after the *vomir* incident, and I found that Mum was out and I couldn't get in the front door. I tried wiggling my key around, checked to see whether some local yob had put glue in the lock for a laugh and was watching me struggle from behind a parked car, or whether in my sick and tired state I was actually trying to use the wrong key or even get into the wrong house. Even the side gate was locked. Someone, it seemed, had changed the locks.

So here I am, sitting on the top step, huddled into my coat, waiting for Mum to come back from picking Jack up from school. This is *so* not the glorious end of school and beginning of half-term I had imagined. I think about walking towards Hilmartin Junior School to find Mum and the keys, but decide I can't be arsed and just lean against the front door.

'Sorry!'

I must have been snoozing and I've woken up to find Mum trudging up the steps in her coat and pink wellies, a sour-faced Jack ambling behind her. I think he's pretty miffed that he's being escorted to and from school like some sort of prisoner, but it's his own fault. Mum leans over me and I look up to see her sticking a shiny silver key in the lock. 'I thought I'd be back before you. I've got you a new set of keys.'

I roll away from the door, pull myself to my feet and follow them into the house, taking off my coat and throwing it over the end of the banister. We've got a coat rack, but somehow I *never* seem to manage to stretch my arm up to use it.

When I turn round, Mum is locking the front door from the inside. I notice there's a thin band of pale skin where her wedding ring has been for the last fourteen years. She steps out of her wellies, and when she takes her coat off I see she's still wearing her red tartan pyjamas.

'Why are the locks changed?' I ask as I follow her down to the kitchen. 'And why have you locked the door from the inside?'

'I'm trying to keep Jack in, and your father out. I don't want *that man* just coming and going like he used to,' she replies. 'In fact, I don't want him coming here at all.'

I slump on the sofa and kick my shoes off. They skid across the floor and stop under the telly.

'He rang me at school today.'

Mum says nothing but starts to pour herself a huge glass of red wine, though it's not even four o'clock.

'Dad. Dad rang me at school today,' I repeat.

Mum takes a gulp of the wine, tops up her glass and says icily, 'I'd rather you didn't talk to your father, Electra, but if you do I don't want to hear about it and I don't want him near Jack.'

I *so* don't want to speak to Deceitful Dad, but I think it's unfair for Mum to keep him and Jack apart. It's not so bad for me as I have a moby so if I want to ring Dad at two in the morning and scream obscenities down the phone at him for leaving us, I've got that choice. Jack doesn't.

'Anyway, you can't lock the front door from the inside and keep the key,' I whinge. 'It's dangerous. What if there's a fire in the night? We won't be able to get out.'

'Use the back door,' Mum says. 'I've locked the side gate, but you could get out into the garden.'

'But what if we *can't* use the back door? What if the only way out is the front door because the back door's on fire?'

'Then I'll unlock the front door!' Mum's voice is getting taut with irritation, but I can't help pushing her.

'Oh, great!' My voice is sing-songy and sarcastic. 'You can hardly even find your own car keys! I'll be burning to a crisp whilst you're looking in your bag going, "Now, where did I put those keys?"'

'Electra . . .' Mum's voice has a warning tone, but I ignore it and plough on.

'Jack and I will be just little piles of ash and teeth and they'll only know who's who by our dental records and . . .'

'SHUT UP!' Mum screams as her wine glass whizzes past my ear. 'WILL YOU JUST SHUT UP!'

The glass shatters against the wall next to the sofa, and we both stare as the red wine drips like watery blood down the magnolia paintwork, *horrified* at what has just happened. Before Dad left, Mum barely even raised her voice to me and now she's hurling alcohol-filled glass missiles in my direction.

'I'm sorry,' I say, shaking. 'I shouldn't have wound you up.'

'No, *I'm* sorry!' Mum comes over and hugs me. She's crying, but although I'm desperate for a sob my tear ducts remain on shutdown. 'We'll get through this, Electra, I promise. Everything will be OK. *Believe* me.'

I'm not so sure. A day into the war and already the troops are fighting amongst themselves.

It's Saturday morning, approximately thirty-six hours since the outbreak of war, and Lucy and Sorrel are coming round. As they are allies they're allowed in the bunker, plus we still have a week of school-free time to plan and a possible *major* problem with the Snogability Scale to deal with. It may need *totally* reworking based on the *horrific* information that Jasmine has passed on to Sorrel, which is that sometimes the lush-looking boys are the worst kissers and the really unfortunate-looking boys are the best. If it's true, this info will turn our S-Scale on its head, particularly as on that basis Freak Boy would score *beyond* a 5. It disturbs me to think of Freak Boy anywhere *near* the scale.

I'm downstairs in the kitchen pouring out a bowl of

Shreddies when there's the sound of scrabbling at the front door. Someone is trying to do what I did yesterday, which is to force an old key in a new lock.

Dad.

He is obviously too stupid to realize that you can't announce you've had a secret trollop stashed away and then expect to keep popping round as normal.

'Leave it!' Mum orders from somewhere in the house.

There's more scrabbling and then the doorbell rings.

Mum ushers Jack downstairs into the kitchen. As the bell continues to ring and Dad hammers on the front door shouting, 'Can someone let me in?' I really do feel as if we're under enemy attack.

The letterbox rattles and I know he'll know we're in because we're always in at this time on a Saturday, and because he'll see our coats hanging over the end of the banister. The doorbell rings again, there's more banging on the front door and then the sound of footsteps running back down the steps.

'Over here!' Mum orders, and without questioning, her troops rush towards her and we flatten ourselves against the kitchen units as the shadow of Dad bending down and looking through the bars on the front basement window crosses the kitchen floor.

I'm not happy about hiding from Dad, and I'm mad as

hell at him, but I daren't risk Mum going nuclear so near to a pile of plates. I don't want more crockery-smashing, especially in front of Jack who looks confused and tearful.

There's silence and the sound of a car driving away. Not a van, but a *car*.

'He's stolen my car!' Mum shrieks racing up the stairs as Jack and I follow her into the front room. The combination of weight loss and being angry with Dad has certainly made her more lively.

We look out into the street to see the space where Mum's car had been parked, now filled by a white pest-control van.

Next thing I know, Mum is downstairs on the phone. 'Police? Yes, I want to report a stolen car. It's just been taken from outside my house, 14 Mortimer Road . . . Registration? . . . No, I don't know the registration but I can look it up. Name? My name is Ellie Brown. I can give you a good description of the thief . . .'

I think Mum's been ridiculous ringing the police but I daren't say so. We're sitting downstairs in the kitchen bunker waiting for them when the doorbell rings.

'Check who it is first,' Mum orders as I bomb upstairs and peer out of the front window.

It's Lucy and Sorrel. I'd temporarily forgotten they were

coming round for a serious bed-blobbing, nail-painting and gossiping sesh.

I go to open the front door but then remember it's locked from the inside and Mum has the key.

'Hang on!' I yell through the letterbox, before haring back down to the kitchen.

'Key please,' I say to Mum, holding out my hand. 'It's the girls.'

She hesitates before handing it over, as if she wants proof that it really *is* Sorrel and Lucy, and not Dad trying to blag his way behind enemy lines disguised as either a black girl with tight braids or a willowy blonde.

When I finally get the door open the front step is crowded with Lucy and Sorrel *and* a policeman and woman.

'Is everything OK?' Luce asks, glancing nervously at the coppers. I'd told her that I'd thought Mum was within a millisecond of stabbing Dad with the kitchen knife when he dropped the Bitch Troll bombshell.

'We've had a report of a car being stolen from outside here,' says the policeman. 'Can we come in?'

The four of them troop in and I show them into the lounge-cum-junk room. There's nowhere to sit on account of the sofa being used as extra storage, so when Mum appears we just all hover awkwardly.

Jack comes belting down from his room. He looks worried when he sees the police and asks them, 'Did you use a siren and lights to get here?'

The policewoman smiles at Jack. 'We walked. Now, if I could just take some details?'

Jack stomps out disappointed that the police don't have flashing lights and sirens on their helmets.

I notice Sorrel is watching the policewoman. She once told me she fancies joining the police force when she leaves school, mainly, I think, so she can arrest people and flash her warrant card around. I can imagine her grabbing some shoplifting kid like my brother and saying, 'You're nicked, son.' And she'd look well foxy in the uniform.

'Now, when did this happen?'

'About half an hour ago,' Mum says. 'From right outside the house.'

I'm looking out of the window and notice that the van that had been parked in the crime scene is pulling out into the road.

'And the car registration number?'

'W982 MWE,' I say.

'What a good memory,' says the policewoman brightly. 'Well done.'

'Er . . . no,' I say, watching a small silver Golf

manoeuvre into the newly vacated space. 'I didn't remember it. Dad's just brought the car back.'

'Dad?' the policeman says, and I turn round to see the two coppers exchanging despairing looks. The policewoman mouths *Domestic* at her colleague.

'My husband, my soon to be *ex*-husband,' Mum says acidly, 'took *my* car without *my* permission.'

The policewoman snaps her notebook shut and goes to the front door. We hear her shouting down the steps, 'Sir? Could we have a word?'

Quick as a flash Mum is out of the room and at the front door shouting, 'Keep that man outside!'

Sorrel and Lucy shake their heads, and I roll my eyes so far back in my head I feel a stabbing pain.

'I just came to fill the car up!' I hear Dad shout. 'I always fill the car up on a Saturday and check the tyres and the water.'

If I'd thought that life would continue as before, but just with the knowledge that Tits Out was right all along and Dad *did* have some totty on the side, *boy* was I wrong.

Chapter Twenty

The girls have gone. I couldn't concentrate on the S-Scale, didn't feel like gossiping and hadn't the energy to paint my nails. They suggested we mooched around the shops at Eastwood Circle to take my mind off things, but the *moment* the police left and Mum realized that Dad had left with a set of her car keys she hared off to Halfords to buy a steering-wheel lock, leaving me strict instructions to keep an eye on Jack. The girls said it was fine, that we could just lie on my bed listening to music and reading magazines, but I felt like being on my own so I said I was tired (true) and that I had a headache (also true) so reluctantly they left, but only once I'd promised on Jags's life to text them later.

I'm lying on my bed, my earplugs rammed into my ears and Green Day at top vol on my iPod, staring at a spider which is walking across the ceiling and wondering why gravity doesn't bring it plummeting down on to my head, when I become aware of an evil force. It's Jack, standing at my bedroom door, staring at me. He doesn't come in. He daren't come in. He knows if he so much as puts a toenail inside my space he's *dead* meat.

I rip out my earplugs. '*What?*'

'Is it true Dad's run away with a mental machinist?' he asks.

'A dental hygienist,' I correct him, although I think his description is better.

'Is Dad going to go to prison like Freddie's dad? Is that why the police were here?' He looks pale and worried.

Freddie Spedding was Jack's best friend until last summer. Freddie's mum, a bank manager for Lloyds (or was it Barclays?) ran off with the bank manager of the local HSBC. When Mr Spedding found out he went round to the HSBC and sprayed: THIS BANK TAKES YOUR MONEY **AND** YOUR WIFE! on the wall outside with a can of silver aerosol paint left over from Christmas. Of course it was all captured on CCTV, and Mr Spedding was arrested and found guilty of criminal damage. He refused to pay the fine and so was sent to prison for a week, which meant he lost his job as a solicitor and now works at Asda on the wet fish counter. Mrs Spedding moved to Wales with Freddie and his sister, Molly, but without the HSBC manager who at the last minute decided to stay with his wife and their prize-winning Persian cats. It was all *such* a mess.

'Not as bad as that,' I reassure him, thinking, *I hope Mum doesn't go to the dentist's and spray: STAFF HERE REMOVE HUSBANDS AS WELL AS TEETH! on the wall.*

Jack doesn't look convinced. He makes a daring move and puts the tip of his left trainer into my room. Usually I would have screamed, 'Stay right where you are, scroat face!' but there are already too many enemy lines in this house.

'Is it my fault?' he asks. 'Are they splitting up because I stole those things?'

I shake my head. 'They'd already decided to separate before that.'

'Well, what *did* I do?' His bottom lip is quivering. 'I must have done *something*. I heard them shouting about me nicking stuff.' He starts to cry big fat tears. 'I'll stop kicking my ball against the fence and pick my pants up!' His whole body is shaking. 'Electra, ring Dad and tell him I won't do anything bad *ever* again. *Please!*'

I get off the bed and do something I *never* do unless I'm ordered to by Mum when she's taking photos to send to Aunty Vicky or Grandma. I go over to Jack and give him a hug.

'You should talk to Mum,' I say as he sobs into my stomach.

'She's not like Mum any more,' he snivels. 'She's mad all the time. I want the old Mum back and I want Dad back here.' When I realize his nose is running I decide the hug has gone on long enough, and I gently push him away, checking that he hasn't snotted on my top.

'Look,' I say, remembering the reframing article about seeing situations differently, 'there are loads of advantages to your parents splitting up. Masses and masses.'

'Like what?' Jack doesn't look as if he believes me.

I'm stumped for a moment. 'I'll write you a list.'

Good Things About Being From A Broken Home

1. Two sets of Christmas presents.
2. Two sets of birthday presents.
3. Two lots of Easter eggs.
4. Two holidays e.g. trips to Disneyworld Florida *and* Paris.
5. If you fall out with Mum you can storm off to Dad's.
6. If you are annoyed with Dad you can come back to Mum's.
7. Dad will feel so guilty about leaving he'll let you get away with murder and buy you anything you want,

within reason, e.g. he can't afford to buy you the Arsenal team to play footie with in the back garden.

8. Mum will feel so sorry for you she'll let you have anything you want for tea, even if it's Pot Noodles five nights running. This may not last long so enjoy it while you can. If she feels sorry for me, she might buy me a pupster.

9. If you get into trouble at school, don't finish a project or forget to hand homework in, look tearful and sob, 'My parents are separating.' Should work for a bit. Note: This sounds pathetic if you use this excuse for years.

I finish the list, go downstairs and push it under Jack's door. I hope it makes him feel better.

I don't believe a single word of what I've written.

Chapter Twenty-one

I lie in bed, wiggle my toes and look at the clock. 10 a.m.! I'd hoped to sleep in longer, maybe even until lunchtime, but I had a *really* weird dream which woke me up with a fright. My heart's only just stopped hammering underneath my Snoopy nightie.

I dreamt that I came home from shopping to find the locks had been changed *again*, but this time it was Dad and The Bitch Troll who were inside, and Mum, me and Jack were stranded outside on the pavement in the pouring rain. I could see The Bitch Troll at a window, waving at me, looking all triumphant that she'd got Dad *and* the house.

No wonder I'm having dodgy dreams. So far half-term has been *terrible*. I've been stuck with looking after Jack whilst Mum's been to visit a solicitor, the bank and the doctor. She's given up the cabbage soup diet, instead she's drinking lakes of red wine. The house no longer stinks like a cabbage patch, instead it reeks like a brewery. If Mum turns into a liver-failing alky with a red nose and bloodshot eyes because Dad's shacked up with The Bitch Troll, I'll *never* forgive him.

Living in a war zone is the pits. Dealing with Mum is like walking across a field full of hidden landmines. Even when she seems OK on the surface, the atmosphere is permanently tense, and then suddenly, *Bang!*; without warning you've said the wrong thing and she explodes with anger, ranting and raging for hours.

As is usual in times of war, communications with the outside world are restricted.

Nana Pat has tried to ring, but Mum slammed the phone down on her. Nana then left a message for Mum to phone her, as did Dad, so the plug for the answerphone has now been ripped out. We're instructed to screen the calls before answering the phone, and there's a list of enemy numbers stuck to the receiver for handy reference. I don't know what Mum's said to Grandma, or whether anyone's rung Aunty Vicky in New York. I do know that Mum's been on the phone to her friend from school, Jan, who's now living in Sydney, Australia. I know this because when I can't sleep I've crept downstairs late at night and heard Mum sobbing down the phone. There doesn't seem to be much actual conversation, just a series of sobs and gasps and watery snorts and empty wine bottles on the side the next morning.

Still today, Valentine's Day, Wednesday 14th February, I'm let out of the bunker. Jack is at football at the sports centre, Mum has *another* appointment with Burrell & Co., her solicitors, and I'm going shopping with the girls.

Sorrel, Lucy and I have arranged to meet outside Debenhams at Eastwood Circle but not until two o'clock as Lucy's post doesn't come until late morning, and as the childminder is ill Sorrel has been lumbered with picking up the twins from morning nursery and taking them to The Bay Tree. She's *furious* that Jasmine refused, saying she had to study for her mocks and couldn't be disturbed, which Sorrel says is just an excuse as she's happy to be disturbed if one of the sixth-form boys comes sniffing round.

Before I go out there's some serious getting ready to do as half the school will probably be mooching around the shops and I don't want anyone to see me looking daggy. I'm not going to pull out *all* the stops because yesterday Lucy texted me some *terrible* news. Jags is out of the country! He's gone skiing during half-term! I think of all those foreign foxes (French or Italian? Defo exotic) helping him to carry his skis or giving him extra tuition in how to bend his knees, and even though I'm bursting for a pee I pull the duvet back over me. I think I'll just hibernate for a bit longer. Life's hard enough without having to cope with cross-Channel competition for The Spanish Lurve God.

I had a little more light snoozing rather than deep sleeping, but now I'm hungry so I'm still yawning when I stagger downstairs in search of a Pop-Tart to toast.

A pink envelope with a printed label addressed to me is lying on the doormat in the hall.

I don't jump with joy and my heart doesn't flutter as I know it's not a proper lurve-card, but communication from behind enemy lines.

A Valentine card from Dad.

He's got a nerve after all that's happened.

I sneer at it, stamp on it, pick it up and drop it unopened on the table by the front door and then go and have breakfast.

I have a strawberry Pop-Tart and then, to cheer myself up, a chocolate one, then I go back upstairs to get dressed, which takes *ages*. I eventually decide on moderately trendy jeans, a white T-shirt under a khaki-coloured jacket which I feel suits the military atmosphere, a big muffin-top-disguising belt, and some brown boots which really need cleaning and reheeling, but have been neither clean nor fully heeled since the day they were bought.

By the time I get downstairs the fact that Dad even dared to send me a card is really bugging me. I rip the envelope open and pull out the card. It's a picture of two cartoon bees kissing and inside is printed *Bee Mine* with a handwritten *x*.

Pure cheese.

I wonder what he's written inside The Bitch Troll's card and feel ill.

I grab my bag, and as I leave the house I tear the card up into masses of tiny pieces like cardboard confetti. I'm *so* not a litterbug – it sends me mental when I see people chuck litter on the street – but in a rare act of totally antisocial behaviour I toss the confetti-ized card up into the air and watch as the scraps flutter down on to the pavement and blow away in the icy February wind.

'So how many did you get?' I ask Lucy. She said on the phone she was getting a cold, and she's looking red-nosed and snotty standing outside Debenhams.

'Five!' she says, patting her bag. 'And you?'

'One. From Deceitful Dad as usual. It's *pathetic*.'

Sorrel comes racing up, huffing and puffing. 'You

been here long?' she gasps, and we shake our heads. 'The twins were plastered in poster paint when I picked them up so I had to take them home to clean them. Have I missed anything?'

'Luce got five cards and I got one from Deceitful Dad,' I say.

'Just one?' Sorrel asks. 'Are you *sure* it's from your old man?'

'Defo,' I reply.

'Give us a look then.' Sorrel holds out her hand.

'I've trashed it,' I say. 'I don't want anything to do with that man.'

We've haven't been at the shopping centre long, and we haven't bought a bean, but Luce is feeling a bit rough and wants to go home, so we're going back to her house so she can have a Lemsip, and we can have a closer look and decipher of her Valentine cards. We're just heading towards the bus stop when Sorrel and Lucy decide they *have* to go to the loo before they can get on the bus.

'I'll wait here,' I say, as they head off.

I hang around looking in H. Samuel's window, deciding what engagement ring to have when Jags realizes I'm not a non-person, but *the* person. I'm thinking rock-sized mega-bling and dazzling, there being no point in the ring being small and tasteful if you've managed to bag a 5 on the S-Scale.

'Hi-ya, Electra!'

I turn round to see Claudia Barnes coming out of La Senza opposite, heading towards me, carrying a little bag probably stuffed full of silicone chicken fillets to stuff in her bra. 'Did the postie bring you any cards this morning?'

I can't bring myself to say, 'Just one from my lying scumbag dad,' so I casually toss my hair, a disaster as strands stick to my lip-glossed lips, and say, 'Yeah, a few, and one special one. You?'

'Oh, me and Nat went shopping early so I've not seen the post yet.'

The liar! She's trying to make out she's too cool to care, plus there's no sign of a bag-laden Butterface.

I think she knows I don't believe her as she delivers a low and unexpected blow as revenge. 'I expect one of yours is from Razor Burns.'

I'm just about to freak at the thought that she could even think such a thing when suddenly her shoulders jerk back, her tits jut out further and she coos, 'Oh, hi, Jags!'

I am going to faint.

Luce said that Jags was going skiing, but he's not on-piste frolicking with exotic foreign minxes. He's here, standing right in front of me, outside the shop where I've been planning our engagement. I'm just grateful that this time I'm reasonably dressed and not wearing an Arsenal tea cosy on my head, even though the ends of my hair are stuck together, coated with Juicy Raspberry Lipglaze.

'Hi.'

The Queen of Sleaze is obviously *not* a non-person to Jags as he directs this casual sexy *Hi* to Tits Out, not me.

Claudia giggles and waves her La Senza bag at him. 'Do you want to know what I've got in here?'

Jags doesn't look particularly interested, but Claudia doesn't seem to notice. She pulls out a small red G-string dotted with pale-pink hearts, wiggles them in the air and says coyly, 'They don't cover much, but then down there they don't need to!'

I am *totally* shocked. I *so* wish that Sorrel and Lucy were around to see this overt show of slaggery. This is *way* beyond flirting. This is practically lying on the ground waving your legs in the air saying, 'Take me now!'

Luckily Jags doesn't start making out with Tits Out in the middle of Eastwood Circle Retail Park, but just fiddles with the zip on his sweatshirt looking bored, gorgeous and Spanish.

'I *love* shopping, don't you?' Claudia gushes, stuffing the thong back into its bag.

Jags and I exchange glances because neither of us are sure who Claudia's talking to, but the mere fact that Jags and I have locked eyes, if even only for a nanosecond, sends my brain to quivering jelly and I find myself stammering, 'I like this place and willingly could waste my time in it.'

'Oh, right,' says Tits Out. 'Whatever.' She raises the marching eyebrow ants in a way which suggests I really shouldn't be out and about without my name sewn into my coat and a responsible person looking after me. 'Have you bought anything?'

They *both* look at me, and already suffering from Jags-induced jelly brain and the humiliation of using a Shakespeare quote when I didn't mean to I blurt out, 'Nothing. Nothing will come of nothing.'

And then I pray to spontaneously combust.

'Is she all right?' Jags asks Tits Out.

Claudia smoothes her already poker-straight hair and says knowingly, 'She's a friend of James Malone's kid sister.'

'Oh!' says Jags as they walk off together, as if that explains everything.

Chapter Twenty-two

I send Dad an email.

To: Dad
From: SOnotagreekgirl1
Date: 15th February 14.27
Subject: Card

D –
Don't EVER think about sending me a Valentine card
EVER again.
Yours,
E

I press *Send* and then even though I'm annoyed with Dad
I wish I hadn't been quite so rude.

*   *   *

An email comes back quite quickly.

To: *SOnotagreekgirl1*
From: *Dad*
Date: *15th February 14.43*
Subject: Re: Card

Dear Electra,
About the card. Sorry, this year I didn't send you one. With everything that has gone on, I thought you wouldn't want me to.
Can I see you and Jack soon, perhaps for a pizza?
Missing you.
Lots of love,
Dad xx

I'm contemplating spending the rest of the week on my hands and knees in the street, trying to find every tiny scrap of trashed Valentine card as if I'm a detective collecting evidence for a murder, when the doorbell rings. I get the spare key from between the Yellow Pages where Mum thinks Jack won't find it, and when I open the door Bella and Tom Malone are standing on the doorstep.

I'm surprised to see them. The Malones and Browns are friendly, but only in a parentals-at-the-school-gate-or-function-type friendly.

'Oh! Hi!' I say, as I hear Mum clattering up the stairs behind me.

'Bella! Tom! Thanks for coming!' Mum kisses them both. She was obviously expecting them but never thought to tell me.

'How's Lucy's cold?' I ask as we all troop downstairs after Mum.

'Nasty,' says Bella. 'She's streaming. It's just a good job she's getting over the worst during half-term so she won't have to miss any school.'

Tom and Bella stand in our basement kitchen and look around. With their pristine clothes and immaculate hair they look like shiny new pins in a dusty old haystack. Tom has his moby hands-free stuffed into his ear. Bella seems to be wearing extra-sparkly diamond studs in her neat little earlobes.

'Can I just poke around, starting from the top?' booms Tom. 'Get a feel for the place?'

Mum nods. 'Go ahead. As I said to Bella on the phone, I'd just like some idea of what it's worth and then perhaps we can talk about putting it on the market. Coffee?'

'Green tea if you have it,' says Bella, which sends Mum hunting in a cupboard. 'Or Earl Grey, no milk, if you haven't.'

I'm shocked. Not about Bella's choice of snobby

tea, but about what Mum has just said.

'We're moving?' I gasp.

'Possibly,' says Mum, sounding vague as she sniffs a bunch of unlabelled teabags she's pulled from a storage jar marked *Sugar*. 'But in any case, my solicitor has asked me to get an idea of the value of our assets.'

Assets! This house is more than just an asset! It's our home. *My* home. There are marks up the doorframe in the kitchen showing how much Jack and I have grown over the years. Pippin the hamster and several unnamed goldfish are buried in the garden. My handprint is on the patio where I put my hand in some wet concrete Dad was using, a brave move considering how *his* dad died. My room at the top of the house is a little haven, a place away from everyone else where I can dream that I look like Hilary Duff and that Jags is saving himself for me. The bad memories are only recent. For me, this house is bursting with good ones.

I feel even more upset when Bella looks around the kitchen and says, 'I expect Tom's valuation will come in rather on the low side, Ellie. There's quite a lot of work which would need to be done to bring it up to scratch. But if someone did it up properly it could make a lovely family home.'

I've always looked up to Bella, not because she's warm

and friendly like Yolanda, but because she's a grown-up version of the popular Princesses of Cool girls at school. But now I want to frogmarch her out of the kitchen and into the garden, force her to lie on the damp grass with dandelion leaves stuffed into her perfect diamond-studded ears, and let Google out of his hutch to savage her. How *dare* she say, '*If someone did this house up it could make a lovely family home*'? It *is* a lovely family home. It's *our* home. At least it isn't patrolled by The Neat Police, ready to arrest you if a shoe hasn't been put away or you've left a dirty mug in your room. At least I can relax in my own home. Lucy can't.

I flop on the sofa and glare at her. I can hear Tom chatting to someone on his moby as he works his way through the house. He's probably lining up a buyer *right now*.

'We were really sorry about you and Rob,' Bella says.

'What's that?' Tom Malone is coming down the stairs, knocking the walls and swivelling his head around as he does so.

Bella gives a sympathetic little smile. 'I was just saying to Ellie how sorry we were to hear about her and Rob.'

'God, yes,' says Tom, though I can't help wondering if the first thing he thought was *I wonder if they'll put the house on the market through Home Malone?*

He starts feeling the damp patch on the wall behind the pedal bin where the peach stone had festered for weeks. 'I found the whole situation very tough. That husband of yours put me in a difficult position when he came to me about buying the Aldbourne Road flat.'

'Oh! He's buying a flat?' Mum's voice has suddenly gone up a couple of octaves to glass-shattering squeakiness.

'Bought it,' corrects Tom. 'Bought the flat above the dentist's last year. I felt torn loyalties of course, particularly when I realized he was planning to move some woman in, but business is business. The property was proving hard to shift being on a main road with no off-street parking, and it was a cash purchase, no chain.'

I notice Mum's hands are trembling as she pours boiling water into a teapot I haven't seen since Grandma and Granddad came for a visit last summer.

'*When* last year?' Her voice is as shaky as her hands.

'Shall we just leave the tea?' Bella seems nervy. 'It looks as if you've got a lot on your hands, Ellie. Tom and I should be going. Tom, you can get back to Ellie with a written valuation, can't you?' She steers Tom towards the kitchen door, but Jack comes running down the stairs holding his Dalek, blocking their path.

'When did Dad buy the flat?' I ask.

'Tom, we must go! Now!' I think if Bella could have

thrown her hubby over her shoulder and run out of the house she would have done, but Tom stops by the door and looks back. 'He completed last summer, just as the schools were breaking up.'

The *moment* the Malones leave, I go to the computer.

To: Dad
From: SOnotagreekgirl1
Date: 15th February 15.15
Subject: Lies

D –

I've spoken to Luce's dad.
I know you what you did last summer.
I'd rather not see you for a while.
E
/

An email comes straight back.

To: SOnotagreekgirl1
From: Dad
Date: 15th February 15.18
Subject: Re: Lies

Dear Electra,

I'm really upset to get your email. Property is always a good investment whatever the reason.

Just because your mum and me have problems doesn't mean we can't see each other, but if you need a bit of time, I understand. How long do you think is 'a while'?

Love,

Dad xxx

To: Dad
From: SOnotagreekgirl1
Date: 15th February 15.21
Subject: Re: Lies

_____

A while is about the same length as a piece of string.

E

Chapter Twenty-three

I'm gutted that half-term turned out so badly. We had such great plans for the break, but what with my problems at home, Sorrel being lumbered with the twins for most of the week, and then Luce getting a cold, it was a total disaster. On top of that I've been off school Monday, Tuesday *and* today with Lucy's stonking cold. I'm *determined* to go back tomorrow. Being at home instead of being at school isn't all it's cracked up to be, not when the atmosphere is tense, you're not sure when a *For Sale* sign is about to go up outside your house and you've shredded the only proper Valentine card you've *ever* had.

Also, there's been a *terrible* development on the mammary front.

My worst body issue is coming true.

I think I'm developing monoboobitis.

As I felt so snuffly and bunged up I rubbed my chest

with thick Vicks smelly jelly, and as I was rubbing I *definitely* felt that my left boob was *substantially* bigger than the right. I was in bed at the time so I sat up, looked down, lay down, looked down, dragged myself to the mirror inside my wardrobe door and looked sideways to the left and to the right. They *look* about the same, small, but in terms of mass-in-the-hand rather than size-in-the-eye, the right one is *definitely* lagging behind the left by some distance. Either I was right and my mega-hug from Yolanda *did* push them back and only one has popped out, or I am indeed going to have to live with a mono-boob. I could disguise my affliction on a day-to-day basis with a Tits Out-style single chicken fillet in the bra to even them up, but I'd have to pay for two which I think is discrimination against we monoboobites. Also, if I ever manage to get further than a snog and on to the bap-grappling stage, it's going to be one hell of a shock for whoever it is that's doing the grappling. He might think he's wrenched one of my boobs off by mistake.

To try and cheer me up I've had *loads* of texts from Luce and Sorrel.

Luce has apologized for the duff Jags info. Apparently she misheard and it was some boy called Suggs who went skiing, not Jags. I love Lucy, but she's really hopeless on the inside-info front.

Neither of them believe me about the mono-boob issue, but Sorrel says if it *is* true I should apply to appear on one of those Medical Mystery programmes and try and make some money out of my freakish affliction.

But despite the texts I still feel left out and miserable. The cold is better today, the snot's not so runny and my brain feels less foggy, but I've had too much time than is healthy to lie around on the sofa with a tissue stuffed up my raw nose, feeling my odd boobs, going over things in my head a squillion times.

The shocking truth isn't so much that Dad has found someone else and left home – that happens all the time – but that he's lied, not just once, but again and again. He's been living a whole double life behind our backs, going out with The Bitch Troll, buying a flat with her, pretending to live at Nana Pat's, making out he was leaving just for some time and space to get over his mid-life crisis. None of it was true. *None* of it! He didn't tell a little porky pie, a mini picnic one-bite version, he told a massive catering multi-portion-sized one. It makes me wonder if you ever *really* know someone as well as you think you do. Perhaps lots of perfectly ordinary people are walking around carrying these big secrets, lying to their friends and family, or if not exactly lying, forgetting to admit that they have a secret parallel life.

I haul myself off the sofa and trudge upstairs to the living room, power up the computer, and open the email Dad sent me when I'd asked him outright if he had a girlfriend. It doesn't say *You're my number one girl*, or *What a daft thing to say!* or any fudgey ambiguous statements. It says *Of course I haven't got a girlfriend*. I've looked back at it loads of times. Even printed it out. Every time I think about it I'm *sure* that there must be something I've missed, some tiny little detail that Dad slipped in, trying to tell me the truth but letting me down gently. Except there isn't.

I leave the computer running, go back downstairs and flop on the sofa and think about what Angela Panteli had said about all the people she'd seen conducting their secret affairs in The Galloping Greek. I think about Mrs Spedding and the bank manager who also had a wife, and the fact that Freddie and Jack are now hundreds of miles apart and having to make new friends. I remember what Claudia said about her mother and father, and how she now has a father and stepmonster, and a mother and stepführer and all sorts of halfbrothers and stepsisters. Then there's Sorrel's mum and dad, who weren't married but as good as. And now Dad has left Mum for Bitch Troll Baxter.

Yes, I now know her surname, because when Mum

went out, I looked up the Aldbourne Road dentist's in the Yellow Pages and rang them. I used my moby so there was no fear of Mum going through the phone bill with forensic precision, finding the demon dentist's number and demanding to know what I was doing ringing an enemy stronghold.

With being bunged up with my cold I didn't even need to disguise my voice, not that they'd know me anyway. I just said, 'I need to make an appointment with your dental hygienist Candy Smith.'

I was shocked at how easily I could lie. Perhaps it's not only Mighty Mammaries and man-boobs that can be inherited, perhaps there's a Deceitful gene.

'Oh, you mean Candy Baxter,' the woman's voice corrected.

I slammed the phone down, congratulating myself on the crafty way I'd easily outfoxed the enemy to get the surname info, but about two milliseconds later I realized I'd made a mega mistake. Now The Bitch Troll has a surname she seems even more real, and I can't get an image of her out of my head. I know that Ange said she was ordinary, but in my mind she's like an older version of Tits Out, enticing my dad with her shag-me eyes and short skirt, taking advantage of a man when he's helpless in the dentist's chair.

I feel depressed and restless. To take my mind off my mismatched boobs and the trail of relationship destruction flowing through my butterfly brain, I pick up a copy of *heat* and begin to flick through it. It's all about break-ups and make-ups and break-ups again, and all the women have matching breasts. What hope is there for me, a non-celebrity with dodgy-sized baps? Thank goodness I didn't use my building society money for a private detective as I may need the cash for surgery to inflate my right boob.

I switch the television on. There's an audience full of people shouting at a scrawny man covered in tattoos sat between two identical miserable-looking porky women wearing overripe-banana-coloured velour tracksuits. The caption on the screen reads *My twin slept with my hubby!* One of the banana-yellow porkers is bleating, 'I'm just so embarrassed. I don't want anyone to know!'

'You're on national television, you stupid cow!' I yell at the screen. 'Everyone knows!'

One of the women starts crying. I'd *so* love to cry. I've got tears brewed and ready to go, but they won't come out. I'm a bit worried the pressure of so many backed-up tears will eventually cause my eyeballs to pop out, and water will spurt everywhere. This is bound to happen at some critical moment such as when Jags walks by. At least he'd notice me. You can't ignore someone if they're standing with no eyeballs and water jetting out from the empty sockets.

From the sofa I can see Google in his cage in the back garden. He's scowling, looking trapped, angry and ready to lash out at anyone who comes near.

I know how he feels.

I can't stand the scrawny TV sniveller, her sister or her hubby any longer. I want to slap them all, even the guy whose programme it is. I switch off the telly and fling the remote on to the floor, causing the back to come off and the batteries to pop out and roll under the sofa.

Then I don't know what to do next.

I look at my watch. Sorrel and Lucy will be in English with Frosty the Penguin so there's no point in starting a text conversation with either of them.

I could try another TV channel but the thought of pushing back the sofa to get the batteries seems too much of an effort.

I've given up with *heat*.

I have a quick feel of my boobs, feel even more depressed and decide to go to bed, not because I need to, but because I suddenly can't bear the thought of Mum coming back in from the solicitor's and starting another rant about what a lowlife louse Dad is and how she'd be better off if he was dead as then she'd get all the money and none of the aggro.

I trudge up the three flights of stairs to my room and shut the door. I ram my iPod into its speaker dock, set it to shuffle, and decide that as Mum is out and I don't care about the neighbours, I'll pump up the vol to max.

As the walls vibrate with the sound of guitars and I'm about to throw myself on my bed in a suitably melodramatic fashion, even though there's no one around to see me do it, I notice the pile of Christmas photographs I'd printed out. I haven't looked at them since the night I went round to Freak Boy's.

I begin to flick through them.

Who says the camera doesn't lie?

This looks like an ordinary family having an ordinary Christmas. Would anyone have guessed that the paunchy slap-head with moobs was living a double life with a Bitch Troll, possibly even having two Christmas dinners? When he left his turkey and trimmings was he really going out to a plumbing problem, or was he going back to his love shack for a Christmas quickie?

I rummage on the top of my chest of drawers, grab my nail scissors and begin to frantically cut Dad out of every photo, stabbing through the thick glossy paper as bits of his body fall on to the floor. When I've finished mutilating the snaps I spread them out on my bed and stare at them. At first glance, with the multicoloured duvet cover behind them, they look complete. Just bright happy snaps of a bright happy family Christmas. But look closer and you notice the jagged silhouette where Dad used to be.

''Cause everything's made to be broken . . .' sing The Goo Goo Dolls, and I feel my knees buckle from under me, and I sink on to the rug beside my bed, bury my face in the photograph-strewn duvet and howl for hours.

Chapter Twenty-four

'I wish I knew who that card was from,' I say as Lucy, Sorrel and me huddle in our usual place, the wall between the science block and the main school. 'I've been thinking about it all week.'

I still don't feel a hundred per cent and every time I blow my nose masses of thick yellowy-green snot comes out, but I was desperate to get back to school and normality.

'Jags?' Lucy suggests. 'You never know.'

'Oh, look!' I say sarcastically, pointing upwards. 'There's a pig flying across the school field.'

As Jags doesn't even speak to me and hardly looks at me, I doubt very much that he would go to the bother of sending me a card. Not that I care now anyway. I'm *beyond* Valentine cards.

'Does it matter who sent it?' Sorrel says. 'At least someone did.'

'I need to know who sent it so I can go up to them and tell them to go and boil their heads *and* their butts,' I say crossly. 'I'd do that even if Jags had sent it.'

'No, you wouldn't!' Lucy says. 'Especially not Jags.'

'I *so* would!' I snap back. 'I'm fed up of men and their shabby tricks. Suppose Jags and I did start going out? He'd probably be going out with Tits Out behind my back and Butterface behind *her* back!' I blow more bogeys into a tissue. 'The male species is a total waste of space. A chromosomal catastrophe.'

The bell goes for the next lesson and Freak Boy scuttles towards us. I put my foot out to trip him up, but as he keeps his head down all the time he sees it and stops.

'Did *you* send me that card, Freak Boy?' I sneer. 'That Valentine card?'

'Electra!' Lucy cries. 'Stop it!'

I've broken our unspoken code. *The Bitches Not Bullies* code. It's OK to call Freak Boy Freak Boy behind his back, but until now I'd never been so cruel to use it to his freaky beaky face.

'I . . . I . . . didn't send you a card!' FB stammers. He tries to get past me, but I stand in front of him, challenging him, daring him to try and push me out of the way.

'Listen,' I growl. 'Don't you even dare to think about

me, not even in your dirty little dreams. *Understand?*'

'Leave him alone!' shouts Sorrel. 'Stop bullying him.'

'Excuse me!' I snap at her, stepping away to let FB scuttle past. 'Since when did *you* start being Miss Goody Two Shoes?'

'Stop it!' Lucy shrieks. 'Electra, what's got into you?'

'And you can keep out of this too!'

'What?'

'This is between her and me,' I shout at Luce.

'What's between us?' Sorrel says, bewildered. 'What have I done?'

'Nothing!' I shout. 'That's just it. You've done sod all! My dad's shacked up with some tart, and just because *you* didn't care when your dad left home you think I can carry on as if nothing has happened. You're gloating that you were right and he had some tart from the start!'

'You don't know anything!' Sorrel snarls. 'You're supposed to be my best friend and you know f-all!'

'Stop it! Stop it!' Lucy shouts. She's in tears and ripping great chunks of skin from her fingers with her teeth.

Sorrel and I stand glaring at each other.

A tall good-looking black girl with straight glossy hair pushes her way through the crowd of kids that have gathered hoping for a fight. It's Jasmine. She strides forward and grabs Sorrel by the shoulders.

'What's going on?' she asks, shaking her younger sister by the arm. 'You causing trouble?'

'Why is it always me who gets the blame?' Sorrel yells, breaking free from Jasmine's grasp. 'The bloody lot of you can go to hell!'

I feel *terrible*.

The row with Sorrel sort of erupted out of nowhere. I'd taken all my anger and frustration and hurt and resentment out on her. I was a mega-bitch and *bang* out of order.

She wasn't in final reg and Frosty got her feathers in a flap and starting squawking, 'Has anyone seen Sorrel Callender?' again and again, until I put my hand up and said, 'I think she had a doctor's appointment,' just to try and keep her out of trouble. Lucy kept giving me puzzled disappointed looks, and as we left school Freak Boy practically cycled in front of a bus to get away from me.

I've tried to ring Sorrel's moby, but just keep getting her answerphone. At about the millionth time of trying I left a message. 'Sorrel. It's me, Electra. Ring me. *Please*.' But even though I've kept my phone near me all evening, *and* sent her a text saying the same thing, I've heard nothing.

I look at the geography homework Buff Butler has set us, but can't concentrate and start doodling in my exercise book. It's going to take a lot of Tippex to white-out *Jags luvs Slags* so that Buff doesn't see it.

My moby vibrates. A text message. From Sorrel!

Can u come out?

I quickly text back: When? Where?

A message comes straight back: Now Outside

I look down into the street from my bedroom window, and when a car comes down the road, in its headlights I see her, sitting on the bonnet of Mum's car. I scurry downstairs, grab the key from the Yellow Pages, unlock the door, and slip outside.

'Do you want to come in?' I say when I get into the road. I'm a bit nervous that she'll start having a go at me and then I'll have a go back and then we'll start to fight without anyone like Jasmine around to break it up.

'It's OK,' she says quietly. There's a pause. 'I just wanted to say . . . I'm sorry.'

'No, no, it's me that should be sorry!' I say. I'd like to give her a hug but unless I climb on to the bonnet she's sitting too far back for me to reach her, and I'm not sure the metal could take the weight of two substantial teenage butts without serious bodywork damage. 'I was a premium bitch. I don't know what got into me.'

'No, I had it coming.' Sorrel's voice is uncharacteristically shaky. 'You were right. I've been a crap friend over all this.

It's just . . .' she hesitates, 'it brought back all the memories of when Dad left and it's been messing with my head again.'

'Again?' I'm shocked. Sorrel has never really mentioned Desmond leaving. She'd always made a joke of it with her impressions of him and the fact that he doesn't ever send her photographs of himself, just pencil drawings, which she says he does to make himself look younger than he really is. 'I didn't think you had a problem with him not being around.'

'Huh!' She gives a brittle laugh. 'How do you think it feels if your dad left you because he'd rather have a goat curry?'

I don't know what to say. The 'Meat or Daughter?' dilemma is not something I've ever considered.

'Are you really pissed with him?' I ask. 'I'm nuclear furious with Dad for messing around with The Bitch Troll.'

It's dark but my eyes have become used to the gloom and I see Sorrel shake her head. 'Nah, I'm not angry at Dad, but I really *hate* Mum for driving him away.'

'No, you don't!' I know her and Yolanda don't get on, but I'm shocked by the venom in Sorrel's voice.

'I do. The Loony Lentil gave Dad an ultimatum. Meat or the family. She didn't try a compromise, say, meat once a week or once a month. She just said, this is how it is and if you don't like it, you can piss off. I think if she'd tried to meet Dad even a quarter of the way he'd have stayed. Or even if she'd said, "Sorry, I've got my potty principles, but let's work something out."'

'Is that why you eat meat? Just to annoy your mum?'

Sorrel shakes her head. 'Nah, it's because I love the stuff. I've probably inherited the meat gene from Dad, but it's even tastier because she's banned it.'

'You should have said something to me,' I say. 'I had *no* idea things were that bad between you and your mum. Look, are you sure you won't come inside?'

'Nah. It's better in the dark.'

I know what she means. Nightmares and worries are worse in the dark. Difficult conversations are easier.

'But things are OK now?' I ask. 'With Ray? I thought he was a veggie when he met your mum?'

Sorrel snorts. 'He is, but *that* relationship will be on the rocks soon. Ray isn't recycling. I've seen him put cans and bottles in the main rubbish. I take them out so Mum doesn't find out, but I can't cover up for him for ever. And there are magazines hidden under the beds in the twins' room. Magazines Mum wouldn't like . . .'

'*What?* Ray's a secret porno perv?' I gasp. 'He's reading mucky mags near the twins?' Ray doesn't look the type to belong to the top-shelf-gazer brigade but, as I found out with Dad, you never really know someone.

'Worse,' says Sorrel darkly. 'Mags like *What 4x4?* and brochures for Toyota Landcruisers. If Mum finds out he's been lusting after Beast Cars there'll be one helluva row and he'll be following Dad out of the door.' Sorrel kicks the bonnet of Mum's car with her heel and I just pray Mum won't notice I'm outside watching her paintwork being trashed.

'Other than being a petrol-head, Ray's OK though, isn't he?'

Sorrel nods. 'He's all right, but I miss Dad.'

'Can't you go to Barbados to see him?' The thought of my dad living in the sunshine with palm trees, golden sands and turquoise seas seems much more appealing than being shacked up with Bitch Troll Baxter in a crummy flat above a dentist's on a main road, but at least he *is* only up the road, not thousands of miles away across the sea.

'Jas would want to come and then I guess Mum would want Senna to get to know him, and we couldn't afford three of us to fly there. Dad says he just needs to sell a few more paintings and he'll try and come over, but the airfares are *soo* expensive.'

I don't know what to say, but I do know that if a

passing pigeon dropped a wad of money into my hands at this very minute, after the initial shock I'd hand it to Sorrel and tell her to get on the next plane to Barbados.

She jumps off the car. I'm alarmed to hear a low twang and wonder if Sorrel's butt *has* made a dent in Mum's bonnet. 'I'll be off then. Just one thing. Don't get all bitter and twisted about your old man leaving. I know I am but it's like a bad habit I can't break. Don't start the habit. Promise?'

'Promise,' I say, giving her a hug.

'Oh and one other thing,' she says. 'Freak Boy didn't send you that Valentine card, I did. Not 'cause I'm lesbionic or anything. Just to cheer you up.'

I know what I have to do as I race towards 7 Compton Avenue. As I pass through the gate, a security light on the driveway flashes on, all 500 watts of it, but I keep crunching up the drive, past a couple of cars and on towards the front door. When I get there another light floods the entrance.

I ring the bell.

Mental muppet dog bounces and barks behind the front door and from inside the house I hear a woman shout, 'Archie! Enough!' before opening it. The woman holding Archie by his collar must be Freak Boy's mum,

226

the doc. She's glam and polished, just the sort of woman who Hot Dad would marry, and I wonder if Lucy's right and FB *was* swapped at birth, and there's some Hot Son sitting in a house of freaky beaky parents wondering, *How did I get here?*

'Is Fr . . . Frazer in?' I say, realizing it's the first time I've ever used his real name.

'Frazer!' Glam Doc calls out over her shoulder. 'You've got a visitor!'

'Do you want to come in?' she asks. I'm almost blue with cold from dashing out to see Sorrel without a coat, so I nod and step into the hallway which is all polished-wood floors and tasteful furniture. FB's parents must be minted.

Glam Doc disappears into a side room dragging muppet dog with her, and FB runs down the stairs. When he sees me he comes to a screeching stop. 'You're not going to have a go at me *again*,' he squeaks, his body hunched over, staring at the floor.

'No! No!' I feel incredibly embarrassed and wish I was having this conversation outside in the dark, but then remember the 500-watt bulbs. I've been too much of a bitch to expect the dark to protect me from humiliation. 'I've come to say . . . I'm sorry. I've been having a rough time at home and I'm just getting over a snotty cold, but that's no excuse for me being a total bitch to you at school.' I finished my gabbled speech. Now it's my turn to stare at the floor and examine the polished parquet.

'I didn't send you that card, you know. I wouldn't dare. You're out of my league.'

'Huh?'

'You're Premiership material and I wouldn't even make it into a Sunday-morning-football-in-the-park-type team.'

'Then you should have sent me off with a red card for bad behaviour,' I say.

I glance up and notice that FB is looking at me and laughing. It's a shock to look him in the eyes and see him happy. I've never even seen the corners of his mouth so much as turn up a millimetre, but when he does smile somehow his features, as odd as they are on their own, work together. And for a nanosecond I know that Hot Dad is *definitely* FB's biological father.

Chapter Twenty-five

Weeks after battle commenced, Mortimer Road is still a war zone and I'm totally battle-weary. There's been no surrender, no ceasefire or even an attempt at a peace agreement. If anything, the war between Mr and Mrs Brown has got worse now solicitors are involved, and I seem to be stuck smack, bang and triple wallop in the middle.

Unlike me, The Little Runt *does* want to see Dad, and Mum's solicitor, Mr Burrell, has made it clear to her that if she isn't to avoid problems with the courts later she *must* let Dad have access to Jack. Unfortunately, as Mum refuses to have any direct contact with Dad, this involves a complicated ritual of bell-ringing and skulking on street corners, the arrangements for which are all done via me and my email account. In our war-torn family email has become the modern-day equivalent of the carrier pigeons used in the war to ferry messages around, and I have become an electronic carrier pigeon.

A typical exchange goes something like this.

Dad sends an email asking me to ask Mum to ask Jack whether he can pick him up at, say, midday on Saturday so that they can go for a pizza or something.

I tell Mum who goes nuclear and complains bitterly about how typical it is of 'Your father' not to remember that Jack will be going to Daniel Finklestein's birthday party that afternoon, even though I doubt anyone has told him and Dad probably doesn't even know who Daniel is, unless Plunge It Plumbing Services has removed an unspeakably foul blockage from the Finklesteins' toilet.

As I sit at the computer, Mum stands behind me barking out instructions such as, 'Will you type: Mum says you can see your son between 9 and 9.30 a.m. on Saturday morning, but only if you confirm, in writing, by return, that you will be on your own at all times.'

In other words, the dental hygienist is forbidden to come within a toothbrush-width of Mortimer Road or Jack.

It sometimes takes several emails before a suitable date and time can be agreed, but can the email pigeon stop flying? Oh no, it's forced to keep flapping its wings, this time to act as a lookout.

When Dad comes to the house at the negotiated pick-up time he has to give three short rings on the doorbell, go back down the steps into the street and stand by his van. I then have to stand at the front door and watch Jack go off and meet Dad, and when Jack is safely in the van and Dad has gone, I have to go back inside and put up with Mum interrogating me over whether I was sure that The Bitch Troll wasn't lurking in the back of the van, lying on a coil of rubber piping until Dad had pulled out of the road.

I have to be around when Dad brings Jack back because Mum won't risk getting even the tiniest glimpse of Dad, which is a shame as she's lost a ton of weight because of the stress, and is looking rather foxy in the body area, even if her face is a bit ropey and baggy-eyed at the mo. At the negotiated drop-off time Mum hides, Dad brings Jack to the front door, rings the bell three times and then goes back to stand by his van, leaving Jack stranded on the top step until I open the door and let him in. Dad drives away and I go back to more 'Was she in the passenger seat?'-style questions.

Poor Jack is then forced to take part in an extensive debriefing session at the kitchen table as Mum gives him the third degree. 'What did you do?' 'Who did you see?' 'Did your father say anything about me?' 'Are you sure you didn't see her?' and so on.

I've had to send emails saying, *Mum has told me to tell you that she's going to bleed your bank balance dry and take you for all you're worth*, moving on to *She won't let Jack see you unless you agree to give her everything*, and even *The rest of your things are in the road*.

After that email, Dad immediately sent round a fleet of plumbers in their vans, and I watched from my room as they scurried along Mortimer Road picking up books, records, odd socks and pants hanging from car aerials. I didn't know whether to laugh or cry.

No wonder I'm totally stressed out. As Christmas ended so badly, and half-term was non-existent on the fun, rest and relaxation front, I *really* need a holiday.

I'd rather hoped we might take up Grandma's suggestion that we go to America at Easter to see the Wunderfamily, especially as I'm thinking more and more about the state of Madison's boobs, and whether she too is experiencing a mono-boob stage. Perhaps she's been a monoboobite for ages which is why she's always holding trophies and pompoms in front of her. It's not because she's proud of her achievements, she's embarrassed about her uneven baps.

As the season of the great chocolate egg-fest got closer I started dropping heavy hints about people at school whose parents had booked last-minute cheapo flights on the Internet, or families who were going away somewhere exotic or even just to Butlins, but my constant prods fell on deaf lugs. Even though I had absolutely no feedback *whatsoever* from my heavy hinting, it didn't stop me fantasizing that on the last day of term Mum would pull a wodge of paper out of her bag and say, 'Ta dah! I know things have been dreadful recently, so as a surprise I've booked us three tickets to New York and we're leaving tomorrow!'

This fantasy was smashed to smithereens firstly when term ended and there was no brandishing of airline tickets, and secondly when I heard Mum on the phone to Grandma snapping, 'Do you *really* think I'm going to fly three thousand miles just to hear Queen Victoria go *on* and *on* about her perfect life, her perfect marriage and her perfect family when I don't have any of those things?'

So that was that. The Brown family, or at least what's left of the 14 Mortimer Road contingent, are staying put for Easter.

Although life at home has been crappola since Dad was exposed as a pork-pier, school life hasn't been too bad, and it's miles better than being at home with Mad Mum.

I've been quite enjoying Buff Butler's geography lessons, and am amazed how much more interesting a boring subject becomes if it's taught by a lush teacher. I think Burke's would do far better in the exam league tables if they sacked all the minging-looking teachers like Frosty and Poxy Moxy, and replaced them with Lurve Gods and Goddesses. The truancy rate would plummet too as everyone would want to go to lessons to gaze at the academic eye candy.

All the girls (probably even the Geek Girls) are in lust with Mr Butler. Tits Out always seems to sit at an angle at her desk with the waistband of her skirt rolled over so it's really short and shows her thighs, and Butterface wears so much make-up on geography days, I've started to call her Double-churned. Even Luce seems to give Buff an extra-wide white smile when he asks her a question, but that may be to deflect him away from the fact that she never knows the right answer.

I've gone back to totally ignoring Freak Boy because I don't want anyone to suspect that I am keeping a guilty secret, which is that for a nanosecond (the smallest amount of time I can come up with) I saw that FB had the *potential* to be a high achiever on the Snogability Scale. This makes me feel wretched and dirty and guilty and unfaithful to Jags, even though Jags is undoubtedly being unfaithful to me.

Neither Sorrel nor I have said anything about the night she came round, and as she's back to her old mega-chip-on-the-shoulder self, it would be as if our conversation had never happened, except for the fact that there *is* a dent in the bonnet of Mum's car where she sat, and I got into serious trouble for leaving the front door wide open when I shot round to Compton Avenue to apologize to Freak Boy for my prime bitchery.

Although it's a pain I'm not spending Easter discussing bras in Central Park with the Wundacousin I'm doing *almost* the next best thing, which is sitting in Bella Malone's large shiny 4x4, speeding up to London with Lucy and Sorrel. Bella has a meeting with some big shot at one of the swanky department stores who might be interested in buying a whole load of antique mirrors she found underneath a pile of straw and cowpats in a shed in France. I can't imagine the perfect Bella even going *near* a poo-filled shed without wearing a head-to-toe germ suit and an oxygen mask, but Lucy says that her mum told the farmer – in perfect French, of course – that she'd give him the money to buy an extra cow if he let her have the mirrors, which now they're back in England and de-pood, are actually worth a herd of posh cows.

Even though I've gone off Bella big time since she dissed our house I jumped at her suggestion that whilst she is in her meeting we might like to go shopping in

Oxford Street – which to us just means Top Shop – and then meet her for lunch. There's a teeny-tiny Top Shop at Eastwood Circle, but it's not the same as visiting the Mother Ship.

Mum wasn't too happy about me going as she now regards Bella as one of the enemy, what with being married to Tom who obviously knew that Dad was forming a love nest with Bitch Troll Baxter. If Bella asks after Mum I'm under strict instructions to say that she's very well and glad that she's no longer living with Rob the Reptile, whereas the truth is she's heartbroken, isn't eating, is drinking too much, from the looks of the bags under her eyes is hardly sleeping and taking happy pills from Dr Chaudhri, which clearly aren't working. Bella *did* ask after Mum the moment I got in the car, but I managed to get away with just a muttered grunt which could mean anything.

'I'll be well gutted if they don't have decent jeans in my size,' says Sorrel unwrapping a stick of gum. 'I'm really looking forward to squeezing my arse into some trendy *deneems*.'

From the back seat I can see Bella glance in her rear-view mirror.

'I think what you meant to say, Sorrel, is that you will be disappointed if you can't find any denim jeans in your size,' she says.

'Yeah, that's what I said,' Sorrel says, chewing the gum. 'Well gutted.'

Bella's neat eyebrows arch in the mirror. 'Lucy, Sorrel has just unwrapped some gum. Can you deal with the debris, please?'

Lucy turns and gives us both a *Sorry* look, and Sorrel scrabbles around her thighs, finds the Wrigley's wrapper and hands it to Lucy. Bella has already pulled out a little drawer in the front of the car ready to accept the 'debris'. I'm a bit nervy that when she's finished chewing it Sorrel will stick the flavourless lump of gum on the back of Bella's seat just for the fun of thinking of The Neat Freak's reaction when she finds it stuck to the grey leather.

The car is pretty swish. It's a large silver Range Rover, and it towers over all the ordinary cars. When Sorrel heard about the London trip she *begged* Luce to ask her mum to pick her up outside The Bay Tree as she knew Yolanda would be horrified to see her daughter clambering into a Beast Car, and probably try to slap a *Gas Guzzler* sticker on it immediately. As it was an early start, the choice between longer in bed and being picked up at home, *or* getting up even earlier to get to the café, was an easy one. Instead of seeing the real thing, Yolanda will have to go into an eco-frenzy at being shown a photograph of her daughter kissing the Beast Car's silver paintwork.

Oxford Street is grubby and smelly. The road is packed nose-to-tail with buses and black taxis belching out fumes, and the pavement is already heaving with people. But after shopping in Eastwood Circle, London feels exciting.

Bella has given us strict instructions. Lucy is to text her when she gets to Top Shop, and if we leave to go to another shop, she must text the name of that shop to her mother *immediately*. We're to all meet back under the gold clock outside Selfridges at one.

I'm desperate to wind up the perfect Bella and dare Luce to text *We're in Ann Summers*, but Lucy reminds me about the home-made sex manual. She's worried that if Bella thinks we're curious about sex shops her mum might try and make the trip *Sexucational*.

As we enter the Top Shop Mother Ship I feel as excited as I used to on Christmas Eve when I really thought that Santa Claus was going to come to the house on a reindeer with a sackful of pressies. It's that same feeling of anticipation mixed with the excitement of not knowing what you're going to find.

Sorrel's already galloping down the escalators, so even though Lucy wants accessories we follow her down.

Packs of teenage girls are roaming about the store, clothes flung over their arms, mobile phones wedged behind their ears as they shriek, 'No! Never! As if!' There are several mothers trailing after sullen-faced sulky daughters who obviously wanted to go shopping on their own, but weren't allowed to in case they spent their allowance on butt-skimming skirts or Playboy gel-filled push-up bras. Even more tragic is the daughter who is hanging round her mutton-dressed-as-lamb mum, dying of embarrassment as Mutton Mum holds up a pair of micro shorts and yells above the music, 'I shouldn't really, but at forty I've still got the legs.' When I overheard that I couldn't help myself and started making baa-ing noises in the direction of Mutton Mum, until Luce dragged me away.

You can tell the out-of-townies like us as we've dressed up to go shopping, but compared to the London girls we look as if we've tried just a bit too hard. They look as if they've only just got out of bed (which, being local, they may well have done) and look crumpled but in a thrown-together cool way. It's urban v suburban in the style wars and, looking around me, urban is winning tastefully manicured hands down.

I look at myself in one of the full-length mirrors, obviously avoiding actually looking at my face, just concentrating on my neck down. I'd thought I looked pretty damn cool (excluding neck up) when I'd stood in my bedroom this morning, but standing in the Temple of Style surrounded by hundreds of style disciples I look like one of those celebrities in a *What Was She Thinking?*-type article. My stripy top which looked vintage in the charity shop where I'd found it now looks just old, shapeless and faded. My belt's too wide, the colour of my jeans too light, my bag plain sad and my black ballet pumps just slightly the wrong shape to be right. Everything about me screams *So last year! So suburban! So sad!* In my room my turned-up jeans looked the biz. Here in the Temple of Style I look as if I'm about to go paddling. I do *not* look like the sort of girl Jags would go out with, but I console myself with the thought that Tits Out and Butterface would look just as last year too, but worse. Sleazers of Suburbia!

I hurry away from the mirror and find Sorrel with masses of pairs of jeans slung over both shoulders, looking for even more *deneems*.

Luce is half-heartedly flicking through a rail of long-sleeved cotton T-shirts.

'Found anything?' she asks.

'There's too much choice!' I moan. 'I feel overwhelmed and wrongly dressed.'

'Let's go back upstairs,' she says. 'I could do with a new bag and some more bracelets.'

Lucy amazes me. She's *never* interested in clothes. I can't remember the last time I saw her trying anything on. Actually, that's not true. She used to be a demon shopper until about a year ago when she just stopped. I have asked her *why* she's gone off clothes, and she said that she had so many already she didn't need to buy any more, which is a really weird thing to say, as having loads of clothes doesn't stop you trying things on even if you're not going to buy them. She always comes into the changing rooms which is useful if you can only take say six items in at once, because then you can use her quota, but given that she's so tall, blonde and completely gorge you'd think she might flaunt her Princess of Cool looks a bit more. If I looked like her I'd strip naked and run up and down Oxford Street shouting, 'Look at me!' Well, maybe not naked, perhaps just in a bikini and then only if it was hot and there was no one else around and I knew I wasn't going to get arrested, but you know what I mean. Luce has a bod to be proud of but never shows it off, whereas Sorrel has no problem about squeezing herself into tight jeans and short tops, and flashing her chromium belly-bar, despite having a bit of a muffin-top situation brewing around her waist and tum.

'If you're not buying anything can I use your six?' Sorrel asks Lucy, grabbing some teeny-weeny-tiny strappy tops, the sort I'd never be seen dead in because of my salami arms and partly faded turdy tattoo.

Lucy nods.

'I'll have a look with Luce upstairs and come back down here, and if I haven't used all my six, you can have whatever's left,' I say.

Lucy and I are rifling through a rack of bags when a woman's voice says, 'Excuse me. I wonder if you've ever thought about doing any modelling?'

I'm buried amongst the bags, but I'm out of the rack like a shot to see a very thin and very trendy woman dressed head to toe in black talking to Lucy. As I had my head in cheap leather and my bum in the air I didn't *really* think the question was directed at me, but even so I feel a millisecond of disappointment that the woman wasn't offering my backside a modelling contract.

'We'd obviously need to talk to your parents, but if you're interested perhaps they could give me a ring?' Thin and Trendy hands Lucy a card.

'I don't think so, but thank you.' Lucy is polite but firm, and pushes the card back in the woman's bony bird-like hand.

'Luce!' I hiss. 'You could be another Kate Moss! Take it!'

She looks embarrassed and starts biting the cuticles around her thumbnail.

The woman holds the card towards Lucy again. She really does have hands like turkey claws. 'Just keep it for another time. Perhaps for when you are a bit older?'

'No, I'm sorry.' Lucy rips a long piece of skin from her thumb and then thrusts her hands deep into her jacket pockets. 'I'm just not interested.'

The woman gives me a disappointed shrug as we watch Lucy practically spring away. I contemplate grabbing the card from Thin and Trendy's claws and asking, 'Will I do?' but decide that the disgusted look she's bound to give me would remain burnt into my memory for ever, and the list of things I might need therapy for when I'm older is already quite long.

We've spent just under three hours in Top Shop and now we're waiting under the clock at Selfridges to meet Bella for lunch. Sorrel's thrilled as she's got two tops and a pair of jeans which she says hug her in all the right places and look 'Well wicked'. Lucy bought a slouchy backpack-type thing and several sets of brightly coloured Indian-style bracelets. I've blown my entire April allowance by buying a belt (which looked great when an urban princess next to me tried it on, but will probably instantly turn into suburban tat round my thick waist), a pair of black jeans which everyone agreed were very flattering, a white long-sleeved T-shirt and another pair of face-elongating (I hope) dangly earrings. I also had my nails varnished at the nail bar (Crushed Plum) which was a *big* mistake as I then smudged them getting my purse out to pay.

Bella has texted to say she's running a few minutes late, so we carry on gabbling about the turkey-claw woman that came up to Lucy, trying to decide whether she was for real or just a front for a dodgy glamour-photo agency, the sort that ask you to whip your top off the moment the camera's pointing in your direction, when I notice a man on the pavement opposite trying to cross the road. He has a wide face, balding mousy-brown hair and teeth which flash in the spring sunlight.

It's Dad.

When I get over the shock of seeing him I realize he's with someone. Clinging like a limpet to his left hand as they try to dodge the traffic is a woman. A plain non-existent-looking woman. *The* woman. Bitch Troll Baxter. Before I can run away and throw myself under one of those long bendy buses, or spin for ever in the revolving doors behind me, Dad spots me. He looks absolutely thrilled to see me and his face lights up in a way I don't remember since I was a little girl. On the other hand it could just be the reflection from his gleaming gnashers.

'Electra!' He drops The Bitch Troll's hand and waves frantically at me, pushing his way through the people waiting on the pavement. 'How fantastic to see you!' He goes to give me a hug. He's wearing the aftershave he had on at Christmas, and I'm upset to feel myself automatically stiffen.

He sees the girls. 'Hi, Lucy! Sorrel! Good to see you.'

Sorrel glares at him, but Lucy says brightly, 'Hello, Mr Brown.' She's always so polite I think my father could be a convicted mass murderer and she'd still be nice to him.

I'm aware that The Bitch Troll is standing next to Deceitful Dad, and now that I've got over the shock of seeing them together I stare at her. I don't make any pretence to just glance, I really check her out, looking her up and down several times. Angela Panteli was right. She's *very* ordinary. Shoulder-length brown hair. Forgettable features. Neither tall nor short, fat or thin. *Pearly* pink lipstick. She could never look like a cool London girl. She has *Suburban Mistress* written all over her matching pink separates.

'This is Candy,' Dad says, and The Bitch Troll giggles nervously. 'Candy, this is my daughter Electra and her friends Lucy and Sorrel.'

'I've heard *so* much about you!' The Bitch Troll twitters. I notice she has lipstick on her teeth, which are a bit on the yellow side considering she's supposed to be an advert for dental hygiene.

I say nothing and Dad says nothing but we just stare at each other as if we're in some sort of trance. Despite being in the middle of Oxford Street with the noise of traffic and people surrounding us, there's a deafening silence between us.

Dad looks nervous. 'So, what are you girls up to?'

I'm mad as hell at him and want to strangle the yellow-toothed Bitch Troll with my new belt, but it must be hard for Dad, not seeing me for ages and then meeting like this. Mum might call him a reptile, but he's still my dad, and underneath the tons and tons of hurt, anger, disappointment and hatred I do still love him, a nano bit.

'We're going to have lunch,' I say.

'Perhaps the five of us could have lunch?' Dad asks hopefully. He looks at The Bitch Troll who nods enthusiastically.

'Can't,' I say flatly. 'We're meeting Lucy's mum.'

'Well, what about another time?' The Bitch Troll trills. 'I think it would be super if we could go out together. I'm sure we'd get along really well if we got to know each other. We've probably got *loads* in common.'

'You think so, do you?' I've already had enough of this woman who broke up our family. I look her straight in her nondescript eyes and say, 'Do you like aubergines?'

The Bitch Troll's face looks like a fruit machine running through a variety of emotions whilst her brain scrabbles frantically for what is the right answer to this weird aubergine-based exam question.

I look at Dad. He knows how I feel about the evil vomity vegetable. He starts to stare at her with fixed eyes, willing her to say, *They are the vegetables of the devil*, but his powers of mind-bending are non-existent as her fruit machine face settles on what she thinks is the correct answer. 'I *love* them. They do a fantastic aubergine dip with pitta bread at The Galloping Greek. Perhaps we could take you and your friends?'

If anyone had asked me four months ago how I would have reacted if I'd met my father out shopping with his bit of fluff, and the fluff had suggested we all went to The Galloping Greek to sample their aubergine dip, I'd have put my Christmas money on me going mental, screaming, bursting into floods of tears, putting a curse on them and having to be slapped by Sorrel to stop me becoming hysterical. But standing under a gold clock on a busy street, hearing this ridiculous Suburban Slut witter on about other aubergine-based meals she's had whilst

Dad looks as if *he* feels like throwing himself under a bendy bus is such a ridiculous situation I begin to laugh.

Bitch Troll Baxter looks flustered and confused. 'Have I said the wrong thing?' she asks nervously. 'Should I have said I didn't like them?'

'No,' I say laughing hysterically. 'You said *exactly* what I expected.'

Chapter Twenty-six

I'm pleased I saw Dad and that woman in London because I realized once and for all that whatever has gone on between the parentals is *nothing* to do with me. If Dad finds a woman who wears pearly lipstick on her teeth as well as her lips attractive, it affects me but it's not my fault. Rationally I always *knew* it wasn't, but there was still this annoying little devil voice in my head taunting, *Perhaps if you'd picked up that peach stone or taken more notice of your dad rather than the television he might have stayed! You forced him into the arms of Candy Baxter!*

Meeting The Bitch Troll has silenced that evil chatter. Now that I've seen her I still hate her, but I'm not afraid of her. She's no longer the older sexier version of Tits Out I had in my mind. Now I see her for what she really is. A silly yellow-toothed aubergine-loving woman with no style and a twittery voice. If I had lesbionic tendencies and I was going to use my S-Scale on her, she wouldn't score above a 1.2. I think Dad could have done better for himself.

I haven't told Mum that I saw Dad and The Bitch Troll in London. It would be like deliberately jumping up and down on a landmine whilst juggling a couple of hand grenades minus their pins. Perhaps it would do Mum some good if she too could face the enemy. Then she'd realize Dad left not because the other woman was prettier, or much younger, or sexier or brighter, but just because *he* decided to. Even though I still don't like it, I feel I'm starting to get used to the situation. I know after more than fourteen years of marriage it's early days, but I wish Mum could start to get herself together and leave me out of the battle between her and Dad. I can't go on like this. I can't go back to school for the start of the summer term still acting as a referee between Mum and Dad, always worried about upsetting one or other of them. Most of the time I feel like I've got a permanent band of steel clamped around my head with the tension.

For me, the final straw came on Easter Sunday. A couple of days before, Dad had emailed me to say that he'd pop round with some Easter eggs for me and Jack, but hadn't specified the exact time, to the minute, when he would be in the vicinity of Mortimer Road. This infuriated Mum who demanded that I *immediately* email him back to ask him when he *would* be round, but Dad didn't reply. This meant that we had to go out for the whole day. We walked round a huge lake, had lunch in a café, walked round it again and then had tea in the same café, just in case there might be a doorstep parental confrontation. When we finally got home, me with a stonking heel blister from trogging around the lake in unsuitable shoes, we found that Dad *had* left a bag of Easter eggs on the doorstep, but the local cats had got to it first and bits of purple foil, chocolate and half-eaten mini-eggs were scattered about and were being picked on, and pooped on, by a flock of starlings.

Mum went nuclear mental. She practically marched me to the computer and barked off an email about how pathetically stupid Dad was not to think about putting the eggs in a cat-proof, bird-proof box, and in the light of the thoughtlessness which led to the Great Easter Egg Massacre she'd have to seriously review whether he could be trusted with Jack during visits. Jack cried at the fuss, I was furious that I'd lost out on my Easter chocolate rations, but more upset that I'd been too weak to refuse to type such a nasty email, just because I was terrified of sending Mum into anger orbit.

After Mum had stormed out of the room, still ranting,

I searched the Internet and looked at various sites giving advice about what to do when your parents split up. The basic advice was to explain to your parents how you feel. Tell them that you're finding things difficult and talk to them about how they could help to make your life easier at this challenging time. *They'll understand and try to help you along the bumpy road called divorce*, the website assured. So I'm going to have a chat with Mum and tell her calmly, rationally and nicely that I'd really rather she didn't always refer to Dad as *That lowlife reptile*, or say to me that the next time she sees Dad she hopes it's in his coffin, and that this carrier pigeon is going on strike.

'How dare you even *speak* to that woman!' Mum screams as the car picks up speed. 'I can't believe you didn't tell me! I bet Bella bloody Malone knew he was in town with *her*.'

'I didn't tell you because I knew you'd freak!' I scream back. I hadn't meant to tell Mum I'd seen Dad and Candy in London, but in trying to explain how difficult I was finding the war between them, it sort of came out.

I thought I'd chosen my place (the car) and my time (just after we'd dropped Jack off at Freddie's grandparents' house as he is staying there with his mum and sister Molly for a few days) carefully, but I was wrong. *Sooo* wrong.

'You should have walked away!' Mum crunches

through the gears and races through a just-turned-to-red light as a man sticks two fingers up at us, understandable as we'd almost knocked him down. 'What was he doing in London with *her* anyway? Spending our money – *my* money – on lacy underwear and swanky hotels, I bet! He never took *me* shopping in London.'

I've really really misjudged things. It's the first time the Controlled Release Information System has let me down, and it's let me down *big time*. My mother has not taken the conversation as well as the website led me to believe she would, and now we're hurtling along a dual carriageway at illegal speeds and I'm convinced she's going to kill us. Jack will inherit my digi camera, my weird dream will come true as Dad and Bitch Troll Baxter will move into Mortimer Road, and I'm going to die a virgin with years of practising kissing on my arm wasted. All that will be left will be some bunches of dead flowers beside the road, tied to the spot where we've crashed.

'Mum, slow down!' I plead as I look over and see the speedo has reached eighty.

She ignores me.

'Mum! I'm just trying to tell you that I can't be pulled in so many directions any more. I'm fed up of being in the middle of all this!'

'Oh, so you're saying this is my fault, are you?' Mum

screeches. 'He runs off and you blame me for the mess. Now you're on *his* side!'

'I'm not on anyone's side! *I'm* old enough to try and cope, but think what it's doing to Jack! Think of Freddie the Firebug!'

Mum slows the car down a bit. When we'd dropped Jack off at Freddie's gran's, Mum had asked Mrs Spedding to keep a close eye on him as she and Dad had separated and it had 'hit Jack hard'. She didn't mention the Tesco Tampax incident, but Freddie's mum had nodded and whispered, 'I understand. Freddie set fire to a neighbour's shed and is having counselling at school. I hope you and your husband can manage a friendly divorce.'

I hear a buzzer. It could have been going on for ages the way we've been yelling at each other.

'What's that?' Mum starts looking round the car, puzzled.

I lean over to look at the speedo. We've gradually slowed down to a much more manageable fifty. But then I notice something on the dashboard.

'Mum, why is that light on?'

'What light?'

'The orange one.'

Mum peers at the dashboard. 'It looks like a little fuel pump,' she says. '*That's* what the buzzer is telling us. I think we're about to run out of juice.'

I sit in the car whilst Mum fiddles about with the fuel cap and the pump, filling the car up.

She comes back from paying with a Flake for me.

'Sorry,' she says as she hands it to me. 'Think of it as an olive branch.'

'I'd rather not eat an olive branch,' I say, unwrapping the chocolate stick, and we both give nervous laughs. As the chocolate crumbs scatter over my sturdy thighs and the car seat I wonder if The Neat Freak ever allows Lucy to eat a Flake in the car. She probably would, but only if there was a portable Dustbuster fixed to the dashboard.

'No really, I'm sorry.' Mum stretches the seat belt over her Mighty Mammaries and after a few stabs manages to click the buckle into place. She starts the car engine. 'I didn't mean to use you to get at your father,' she says, pulling off the garage forecourt and on to the busy road without indicating left. 'It's just . . . oh, it's been hard enough just finding the energy to get out of bed in the morning and keep going without having to deal with *him*.' It's the first time Mum has admitted to me she's been devastated about Dad leaving.

'S'OK,' I say with a mouthful of Flake.

Mum shakes her head. 'No, no it's *not* OK. He's still

your dad, *and* Jack's. I should have remembered that and thought about you rather than me. It wasn't fair. I'm sorry.'

'I thought he was coming back,' I say. 'I really thought he was about to come home.'

I bite into my Flake and give Mum a sideways glance. Her face looks softer, as if she's no longer angry, just incredibly sad and totally defeated.

'So did I, love,' she sighs. 'So did I.'

We sit in silence, and I realize that this is the most meaningful conversation the two of us have had since Mum told me she'd had three miscarriages between me and Jack. It's a good silence. A together sort of silence. A mum and daughter silence.

We've only been driving for about five minutes when the car starts doing weird kangaroo-type hops, and there's a knocking sound as if a tiny child is trapped in the petrol tank and is trying to get out. I look behind me and see a trail of weird smoke as the car wobbles along, and I wonder whether Freddie the Firebug has climbed into the tank and is about to blow us up.

'Mum, what's going on?' I say as the car splutters and slows to a halt. Behind us cars are tooting their horns and trying to overtake. Mum tries to restart the car but it keeps stalling.

I remember yonks ago going to Brownie camp with Brown Owl, a large woman with facial warts and a terrible moustache, and the minibus breaking down on the hard shoulder of the motorway. I *hated* Brownies. I only ever got the minimum number of badges, though Lucy got armfuls. Anyway, Brown Owl put the hazard warning lights on and ordered us all to stand in a field, which was just as well as we were able to watch a silver coach with German number plates plough into the back of the blue minibus from a safe distance.

I swing into action.

Once we find the hazard lights (after having tried the fog lights, cigarette lighter and rear windscreen washer) Mum and I sit up on a grass bank at the side of the road looking down at the sick silver Golf, as if just looking at a car will really tell you what's gone wrong under the bonnet.

'Shall we phone the AA?' I ask.

'I thought we were in the RAC?' Mum replies.

Despite the prospect of being ploughed into by a car that hasn't seen the hazard warning lights I rush down the bank back to the car, grab everything from the glove compartment and scamper back up to Mum.

'It's the AA,' I say, pulling out my moby. 'I'll ring them.'

* * *

I have discovered that one of the most welcoming sights in the world is the sight of an AA van speeding towards you, its yellow lights flashing, when you've been sat on damp grass for an hour breathing in carbon monoxide fumes whilst men in cars toot their horns when they notice your mum's Mighty Mammaries. A couple of cars did pull up and ask if they could help, but we thanked them and told them the AA was on its way. I'm sure they meant well, but both drivers looked total pervs, as if they might have ropes and rolls of duct tape in the boot.

The AA van pulls up and a man wearing a fluorescent yellow jacket jumps out. We're about to come down the grass bank but he waves at us to stay where we are.

'Sorry for the delay, ladies,' he says, running up the bank towards us. He's got a lovely warm smile, very short hair and a sort of neat designer-stubble-type beard. 'Everyone's coming back after the Easter break and we've been busy. Now, what happened?'

'It's really weird,' Mum says. 'We were going along fine, I stopped to buy fuel and a Flake, and then we'd only just got going and the car broke down.'

'So maybe you drank the petrol and put the Flake in the tank?'

It's a weak joke but we both giggle helplessly, relieved someone is going to help us.

'I think I know the difference between petrol and chocolate,' says Mum, still laughing. 'And anyway, this is a diesel car.'

'Ah! But do you know the difference between petrol and diesel pumps?' the smiling AA man asks. 'It sounds to me as if this is a classic case of mistaken identity at the pumps. What we professionals call a mis-fuelling incident.'

I roll my eyes and Mum fishes around in her bag to find the garage receipt. After much rummaging, she remembers she's tucked it into her cleavage and pulls it out with a flourish. It's not for diesel. The smiling AA man is right. She's just bought fifty-three litres of Premium unleaded petrol.

'Oh, no!' Mum wails. 'It wasn't that I didn't know, it's just that with everything . . . my mind . . . damn! Now what?'

'I'll tow you to a garage. The car will be out of action for a while. It could be an expensive mistake.' The AA man has obviously seen it all before.

'But how will we get home?' Mum asks.

'Don't worry,' he says. 'It's part of the policy you took out. I'll get you both home.'

The smiling AA man is called Phil Harris. He's been an AA man for five years and he loves it. Before that he was an engineer in the army. He's divorced, but gets on well with his ex-wife, Debs, has no children, would love a dog but feels it would be unfair as he's out at work all day and sometimes all night, lives in the country, rides a Harley-Davidson and likes heavy rock music. I know all this because I'm sitting wedged between him and Mum on the way home whilst they natter away as if they've known each other for years.

'Won't you come in for a cup of tea and a bit of cake?' Mum asks Phil when he finally pulls up outside our house having dropped the sick car at a local garage.

'I'd *love* to,' he says, 'but I'm still on call and there'll be other damsels in diesel distress to see to.'

'Oh.' Mum sounds disappointed, but then she's always keen for an excuse to crack open the carbohydrates. 'Well, thanks for rescuing us, and if you ever have a breakdown near here, the kettle will be on at number fourteen.'

Chapter Twenty-seven

I don't know whether it's the little green and yellow pills shaped like monster mouse turds from Dr Chaudhri, or the threat of her son turning from petty thief to full-scale arsonist, but Mum has seemed *much* calmer since Easter. She didn't even freak when she got a fixed penalty notice through the post to say a traffic camera had snapped her speeding on the dual carriageway the day I thought she was trying to kill us. She's got the Fern DVD out again and is flinging her arms around in front of the TV. She still won't talk to Dad, but I set her up with her own email account – No1foxymum – so now she can communicate directly with him over solicitors and money and stuff. I can hear her crashing away on the keyboard, sometimes screeching at the screen and cursing *that man*, but at least it doesn't involve me. Sometimes she types for hours – she's obviously still got a lot to get off her massive chest, but as she's hoping to get a part-time job as a secretary and needs to get her typing speeds up it's good practice.

I still haven't seen Dad, although I think I probably will, but not just yet and not if Bitch Troll Baxter is around. I've sent him a few jokey emails and just ignored his replies when he's suggested we go for a pizza. Sorrel thinks it might be a good idea if when I do go out with him she and Lucy come too. I'm not a hundred per cent sure whether this is because she's trying to be helpful or to get a free meat meal, but I think it's probably a good idea just so that it's not such a full-on visit, and if the conversation stops Lucy can keep it going even if Sorrel just glares.

Jack seems happier too. When Freddie's mum dropped him off after his visit Jack announced that Freddie was boring as he'd started watching rugby instead of football, and that Daniel was better fun even though he supports Spurs.

About a week after we broke down I come back from school to find a large yellow AA truck parked in the road, and Mum and Phil Harris, the heavy-rock-loving AA man, sitting at the kitchen table drinking tea. Jack is standing by Phil's shoulder quizzing him on the plastic dinosaurs he's pushing under his nose.

'You remember my daughter Electra?' says Mum.

'Hi!' Phil waves as I clatter into the kitchen and head to the fridge. 'Stegosaurus.'

Before I have a chance to say anything Mum says, 'Phil had to go to a call-out on the bypass . . .'

'. . . and as I finished early I thought I'd take up your offer of a cup of tea! That's a brontosaurus.'

Jack squeals with delight that he's found someone who can identify his plastic prehistoric pets.

'It was Mum's offer not mine,' I say sourly, pouring myself a glass of Coke. The man obviously has no idea that if someone says, 'Stop by for a cup of tea if you're in the area,' they don't really mean it, it's just called *being polite*.

The AA man looks around the room. 'Lovely house you've got,' he says gulping a mouthful of tea.

'We're moving,' I say, even though there's been no more talk of estate agents, and my secret plan to chop down any Home Malone boards that appear outside the house and let off stink bombs during viewings hasn't had to be put into action.

'No! Really! Why?'

Mum looks a bit flustered. 'Well, as I told you when we broke down, my husband and I are getting divorced and

I think the family should make a fresh start. I fancy a change anyway.'

Jack goes to show Phil another plakky dino but I grab it, just to annoy him. We're still grappling over ownership of a pterodactyl when Phil asks, 'How long before the settlement is finalized?'

Mum shrugs. 'I don't know. The ex – well, hopefully soon-to-be ex – only moved out just after New Year's Day. It's all in the hands of the solicitors.'

I notice Phil looks a bit surprised, but recovers quickly and smiles at Jack and me. 'What about you two? Do you want to move?'

'No!' we say together.

Bored of wrestling with The Little Runt, I let Jack have his precious dino back, but not before I've bent its tail, on purpose.

'Well, it's none of my business, but if it's just a change you fancy, you could try something less drastic like a new car. You could do a deal with the garage over the cost of the engine repair if they take it in part-exchange on a new one.'

'Can we get a Ferrari!' Jack squeals. 'Or a Lamborghini?'

Mum laughs. 'I don't think we can afford a brand-new car whilst the finances are still being sorted out, and I'd have no idea what to look for in a second-hand one. How would I know that I've not bought one that's been in a shunt, or got a dodgy engine or something?'

'At your service!' Phil announces. 'I'd be delighted to help you choose.'

'*Please*, Mum,' pleads Jack. '*Please* can we get a Ferrari?'

Mum and Phil are laughing at Jack jumping around with excitement, but I'm just watching the cosy kitchen scene, feeling uneasy, thinking, *What's this impostor doing sitting here persuading Mum she needs a new car?*

'Well, not a Ferrari, but the Golf *is* old and I would like an automatic rather than a manual. The ex wouldn't let . . .' She stops herself. 'Yes, I'd *love* you to help me pick another car, if that's not too much trouble.'

'It would be a pleasure,' he says. 'Saturday morning about ten suit you?'

'Can I come?' asks Jack.

'Of course!' Phil says. 'Electra, what about you? You coming?'

Mum is smiling and Jack is bouncing up and down.

'Sniffing around old cars isn't my idea of fun on a Saturday morning,' I snap, flouncing out of the room.

'Sounds to me like this Phil bloke's trying to get his feet under the table,' says Sorrel as we sit on the top deck of the bus going to school next morning.

'More like his bits in her knickers,' says Tits Out, touching up the white tips of her nails with a Tippex pen.

'Oh, don't be gross, Claudia!' I say, cringing. 'That's just disgusting. He's just being friendly, that's all.'

Tits Out shrugs. 'Look, I know these things. When Dad left, every man for miles came sniffing round Mum like she was a dog on heat.'

'Stop it!' I order her. 'You're really grossing me out!'

'Isn't there some sort of breakdown code?' Butterface asks, chewing gum. Without even looking at the timetable I know it must be a Buff Butler geography day as her face is double-churned. 'Like you can't go out with your doctor, perhaps he's not supposed to go out with someone he rescued.'

'I can't report him for coming round and drinking tea, not when Mum invited him over,' I point out.

'Can you go out with a teacher?' Butterface wonders, and we all think of Buff Butler and sadly shake our heads.

'Don't say I didn't warn you,' says Tits Out. 'Today the kitchen, tomorrow the bedroom and then you'll find yourself with a stepFührer, stepbrats and half-brats. Believe me, I know these things.'

'So are you going with them on Saturday or not?' Sorrel asks.

'As if!' I reply. 'I'm not spending a morning sticking my head in car engines!'

'*Big* mistake!' Tits Out is blowing on her nails. 'You need to be there to keep an eye on them. Newly separated parents are worse than teenagers. You never know what they're getting up to behind your back.'

Phil Harris looks surprised to see Mum, Jack, me, Lucy *and* Sorrel all troop down the steps on Saturday morning. I'd invited – well, told – the girls to come along so they could see The Impostor for themselves and I could get a second opinion as to his motives. Jack's disappointed to find that off duty Phil drives a titchy blue Toyota with no flashing lights on the top. I'm a bit alarmed as to how we're all going to fit in the car.

Phil suggests we walk as it's not far, but I stick out one of my trotters and sneer, 'As if!'

Convinced that we would be driven everywhere, and feeling I needed a bit of a boost, I'm wearing a pair of oh-so-fabulous-but-completely-impossible-to-walk-in silver-heeled strappy sandals, totally unsuitable for doing anything other than posing in. I've hardly worn them since I bought them because even after a few totters they cripple me and rub the backs of my heels, and then it takes *weeks* for the blisters to heal.

'Well, go and change them, love,' says Mum, as we all stand on the pavement looking at the tiny blue car and my vertiginous heels.

'Er, no way!' I say, standing my ground, even though already standing on any ground is proving painful.

Mum gives me a *Don't start, Electra!* look, but doesn't push it as she obviously doesn't want a family confrontation in front of non-family.

'I tell you what,' says The Impostor brightly. 'Why don't I run your mum and Jack to the garage while you and your friends stay here, and then I'll come straight back for the three of you.'

Mum thinks this is a great idea, but I'm not happy with The Impostor being in the car alone with Mum. Jack doesn't count as a lookout as I don't think he's old enough to know what to look out for, so I push Lucy towards the blue midget and hiss, 'Stay with them.' Jack looks thrilled at having the Goddess Luce next to him on the small back seat as they drive away.

Sorrel and I have been chatting about the size of our feet for only about five minutes before The Impostor returns, so I force myself to totter from the bottom of the steps where Sorrel and I parked our butts and climb into the car. I've decided I'm going to make it quite clear to him by staying silent that he's *not* going to muscle in on our fractured family, or, if communication is *absolutely* necessary, say when he asks me a question, I'll adopt the killer combo of a sullen face and monosyllabic answers. Sorrel won't speak to him anyway, so I wonder how he'll cope with two sullen girls crammed into his tiny motor.

When I'm in the front seat I notice The Impostor has a skull and crossbones tattooed on his left forearm. That does it for me. I am *not* going to let a man with a death-head tattoo get anywhere near my mum.

He sees me looking at it and rubs his arm.

'Daft, wasn't it? We all had them done in the army.'

'Huh.'

'You ever thought about having a tattoo?'

'Nope.' This isn't true of course, what with the non-fading henna butterfly, but now I've adopted the monosyllabic approach to Impostor conversation, it's important to cut off any further lines of discussion which might require complicated words or phrases.

'Important exams coming up?'

I'll say one thing for The Impostor, he doesn't give up, or perhaps he's just too stupid to realize I've taken a vow of sullen monosyllabacy.

'Nope.'

This is good. It's like some sort of game show. Beat The Impostor. The prize? Mum all to myself.

269

We park at the garage and uncurl ourselves from the car. Mum is on the forecourt peering into the window of a silver Ford Focus and Jack is tugging her on the arm and whining, 'That's *so* boring!'

A man strides across to us. He shakes Mum and The Impostor by the hand and introduces himself. 'Hi! Simon Woodruff, Sales Manager. Would you like me to arrange a test drive in that little beauty?'

He looks all slimy with his eager looks, shiny grey suit and too-wide purple tie.

Mum nods enthusiastically. 'Yes, please.'

Slimy Si sniffs a sale. 'Brill!' He gives a double thumbs-up sign and I cringe. There's nothing more tragic than adults trying to be hip and trendy. 'My colleague Darren is out on a test drive but he should be back any minuto. If you'd just like to step inside the office we can have a look at your driving licence and just fill out a bit of paperwork and then you can take that silver sweetie for a spin.' He steers Mum towards the office and I wonder if Slimy Si will sniff out that Mum is now a single woman and pounce on her.

The Impostor is looking under the car, Jack is stomping around chanting, 'Boring! Boring!' and Lucy, Sorrel and me are leaning against a green Mini (especially me as my feet are *killing* me) when an enormous Beast

Car, a huge black 4x4 Toyota Landcruiser Amazon bristling with chrome, swings into the garage and stops on the forecourt next to us.

A man who must be Darren, as he looks just like Slimy Si, except younger, jumps out of the passenger side, and from the driver's side a weedy pale man with longish strawberry-blond hair tied in a lank thin ponytail. He looks like a chopstick next to the huge Beast Car. I immediately recognize him. It's Ray Johnson, Sorrel's sort-of-but-not-legally stepfather.

'Ray!' Sorrel gasps. She looks so shocked her dark skin has gone ash grey.

Ray looks as if he might climb back in the car, lock the doors and race away. In Yolanda's eyes he's committed the only sin worse than eating meat. He's been lusting after a gas-guzzling Beast Car and secretly driving it. If Ray had an affair with another woman Yolanda would probably just shrug it off and say, 'These things happen,' but her eco-principles are so strong, so important to her, her partnership with Ray probably couldn't survive his car-infidelity. She'd see it not as just letting her down, but future generations and the planet.

'How could you?' Sorrel snaps. 'If Mum finds out she'll kick you out!'

Ray looks sheepish and starts to twist the gold hoop in

his right ear. 'I didn't mean to,' he says. 'On my way to work I kept noticing her, looking all shiny and gorgeous with an immaculate body, and this morning something just snapped. I just couldn't help myself.' Although Ray looks upset I can't help but notice he's still got one hand on the door of the Beast Car and is lovingly stroking its paintwork. 'Sorrel, I'm so sorry. Don't tell your mum, will you? Please? What she doesn't know can't hurt her. I'll never do it again.'

'You will!' Sorrel is furious. 'Now you've felt the power and the leather under your legs you'll do it again, there's too much temptation!' Her beautiful face is contorted with rage. 'And now I've got to keep *your* secret from *my* mum otherwise *everyone* will suffer!'

She turns to go and I try and catch her arm but she shakes free of me.

'Sorrel, wait!'

She's out of the garage and racing along the street. Lucy hares off after her but I'm stuck as I can't totter let alone run in my oh-so-fabulous-but-completely-ridiculous heels.

I feel *terrible*. If I hadn't asked Sorrel to come with me to check out The Impostor she would never have known what Ray was up to. But, on the other hand, if The Impostor hadn't charmed Mum into changing her car we wouldn't be here in the first place.

Mum has come out of the office with Slimy Si. 'Is Sorrel OK?' she asks.

I glare across at The Impostor, who's now looking under the bonnet of the Focus.

'No, she isn't, and it's all *his* fault.'

Chapter Twenty-eight

Dad and I are sitting having sizzling chicken and beef fajitas in the Playful Pepper Tex-Mex restaurant in town. I'd been rejecting his pizza offers for weeks, but then he mentioned the fajitas and I thought, *Why not?* I didn't invite Lucy and Sorrel in the end. I emailed Dad to say that I'd meet him, but only if Bitch Troll Baxter wasn't there and we didn't mention her, and so I sort of thought I owed it to him to be by myself if he was. Also, I'm still so angry with her I don't trust myself not to ram an extra-hot chilli pepper in her mouth and withhold the water.

We've spent half an hour with me asking him about the business and him going through the *How's school?/Lucy?/Sorrel?/homework?/Jack?/Google?/Nana Pat would love to see you* routine, with the odd 'Has the bathroom tap stopped dripping?' and 'Who's been cutting the grass?' thrown in.

For a man supposedly shacked up in a love nest with

his mistress, he looks *very* unhappy. Perhaps his teeth are giving him gyp again. From the look of his man-boobs he's either put on weight, or his polo shirt is several sizes too small. Perhaps The Bitch Troll is crap at laundry and has shrunk them all in a hot wash, or maybe he's having to do his *own* washing for a change.

I missed his birthday last week, the 8th of May. I wasn't quite ready to see him then. I sent him an ecard, a lizard whose tongue popped out saying *Happy Birthday*. I thought it appropriate as Mum still calls him Rob the Reptile, but not in front of me and Jack, only on the phone to her friend Jan, late at night, when she doesn't know I've crept downstairs and am hanging over the hall banisters. I've picked up all sorts of stuff that way, such as the fact that things haven't been right between Mum and Dad since Jack was born, that Mum rang Bitch Troll Baxter up at work and screamed at her, and that Aunty Vicky and Grandma said they'd been expecting the parentals to split for years.

'Have you got a boyfriend?' Dad is hunched over his plate. His coot-head look has got worse, although by the number of flaky bits of skin clinging to his scalp he's still using the anti-slaphead lotion.

'No,' I say through a mouthful of soft tortilla and chicken.

I'd would *so* loved to have said, 'Yes, I'm seeing a Spanish Lurve God,' but I've only seen Jags from the top of the bus or the front of a car as, according to Luce, Jags and James are doing a few GCSEs a year early and they've been too busy revising for their exams to hang around the sports centre or Eastwood Circle. I'm still having the odd very disturbing thought about Freak Boy too. Sometimes I'm enjoying my current favourite daydream where my limbs are not like mottled salamis, but look like a couple of French baguettes, the long thin golden sort, not the thick doughy variety, and I'm looking foxy and fabulous in a little white sports dress. I've just won a game of fast and furious badminton against Gill Pearce, the school's sportiest girl, when Jags comes up to me and says, 'Electra Brown! I had no idea you could handle a speeding shuttlecock so well,' and then takes me in his arms. The problem is that at that point his face morphs into Hot Dad and then into Freak Boy, so that the beautiful daydream becomes a horrific nightmare as I have to beat off Freak Boy with my racket.

'Is your mum seeing anyone?'

Ooh, sneaky the way Dad slips this into the conversation so soon after talking about my non-existent love life. I'm not happy that The Impostor is around, but I'm not going to let Deceitful Dad know this. I feel that the Mortimer Road troops still need to show a united front, and just because I've been seduced by the thought of Tex-Mex food doesn't mean I'm not still nuclear furious with him.

'Why do you ask?' I take a gulp of water as I seem to have bitten into the sort of chilli I had in mind for The Bitch Troll, and my mouth is on fire.

Dad pushes some peppers around his plate with his finger. He's trying to look casual but his voice is tense and a vein on his right temple is blue and throbbing.

'Whenever I see Jack he's always saying, *Phil this* and *Phil that*. He thinks Phil's the bee's knees. Who *is* this Phil?'

'An AA man,' I say, my mouth just about calming down. 'He rescued us when the old car conked out.'

'It broke down? Why?'

I shrug. 'Dunno. The engine just blew up.' I'm half lying not mentioning the mis-fuelling incident, but I want Dad to think Mum is coping with *everything*, even the car. 'Anyway we've got a new one now.'

'Jack never said.' Dad raises his eyebrows, and I've an awful feeling that now Mum has stopped pumping Jack for info, Dad has started.

'It's a silver Ford Focus automatic. Mum loves it but Jack thinks it's boring, which is why he probably hasn't mentioned it. He wanted us to get a red Ferrari.'

Dad doesn't laugh. 'So *that's* why the Golf hasn't been parked in the road. I've been wondering where it was.'

'Have you been spying on us?' I ask.

'Just keeping an eye on things.' He looks even more miserable. 'So this Phil is round a lot then?'

'Off and on,' I shrug.

More on than off, I think to myself.

So far Phil's mended the fence which was wobbly because of the battering it gets from Jack's football and the weight of next door's monster moggy; made a large run for Google so that the poor guinea pig can stretch his spindly little legs in the watery sunshine; sorted out the damp patch behind the pedal bin in the kitchen; cut the grass; stopped the bathroom tap dripping and removed a ton of smelly leaves from the guttering. Despite him being around a lot I am extremely proud of the fact that not *once* have I broken my vow of sullen monosyllabacy.

Jack has already made it quite clear that he would rather spend time with DIY Dynamo Phil than Dad. Phil takes time to play table football with Jack, shows him everything in his toolbox and can talk about sport. It's hard for Dad and Jack as they can't see each other at the house, Dad is forbidden to take Jack back to the love nest to make him a Pot Noodle, and Mum still sees Nana Pat as the enemy and won't let him go there. Any contact with Jack seems to involve trailing round the streets and eating lots of burgers. Jack says going out with Dad is 'Boring and weird'. Sitting in The Playful Pepper I know what he means about the weird bit, it's like going on a date with your dad, and it's a bit sick that it's the only sort of date I can get.

'But is your mum actually going out with him?' Dad presses.

I shrug just to keep Dad guessing. In truth there's not been a hint of romance between Mum and The Impostor, even though I've been on high alert, watching them like a hawk for signs of secret hand-holding or furtive footsie under the table. As I'm still angry with Dad I throw in, 'He rides a Harley and he's got a death-head tattoo,' just to wind him up further.

'I'm not happy about what's going on, Electra.' Dad sounds disapproving, the same way he used to sound when he was talking about my school report. 'Your mum is very vulnerable at the moment and I don't like to think of someone taking advantage of her so soon.'

I'm *mega* furious. It's obviously OK for *him* to run off with someone whilst he's married, but now he's gone he expects Mum to live like a nun. I mean, *I* expect her to live like a nun, at least for a while, but I don't think Dad has any right to.

'What's it to you if she's working her way through the entire fleet of AA patrolmen and then starts on the RAC?' I snap.

'Well, I think it is my business if some man is encouraging my wife to spend my money!'

'She's only your wife on paper and she's going to get a job so if she wants to buy a Ferrari and have a tattoo on her butt that's up to her!'

There's a long awkward silence and for a moment I consider going to the loos and sending Sorrel and Luce a text asking them to accidentally-on-purpose meet me at the restaurant, but then Dad asks for the bill.

'Dad, Mum's just trying to get on with her life,' I say. 'She's had to. We've all had to.'

Dad says nothing. He looks a bit like Mum did during her zombie phase, sort of lifeless and hollow-eyed but with big boobs.

'You wanted this. It was you who went off with . . . Candy.'

Funny that it was me who didn't want to talk about The Bitch Troll, but I'm the one who's brought her name up.

'Don't you think I don't know that?' Dad says heavily.

A sulky-looking waitress with a weeping cold sore hovers by our table with the bill on a white plate. Dad takes it, glances at it and then snaps his credit card on the plate. I wait until Cold Sore Girl has shuffled off and then say acidly, 'You thought the grass was greener on the other side and so you hopped over the fence.'

Dad glances up at me. There's tears in his eyes. 'I know that. But before I jumped, I didn't notice the weeds.'

Chapter Twenty-nine

I'm lying full-length on the sofa downstairs, stretched out so that The Impostor is having to perch on one of the hard kitchen chairs. I'm pretending to read *Teen Vogue*, but really I'm covering my face to disguise the fact that I am nuclear-level furious that Mum and The Impostor are going out for a meal on a *Saturday night*. If that's not a date then I don't know what is, but the worst of it is Mum asked *him* out, the brazen hussy! They're going to La Perla, an Italian restaurant in town which I've never been to but I bet is full of dark corners and dripping candles.

She *says* that she suggested a meal to thank him for all the jobs he's done around the house, but he was obviously pretty keen to accept, as he's in the kitchen, sitting in smart clothes, reeking of aftershave, waiting for Mum to come downstairs. Jack has been farmed out to the Finklesteins' for the night with strict instructions to keep the front door locked, and although I was supposed to be going with Sorrel to hang out at Lucy's I've invited them both here to sleep over instead. Luce jumped at the change of plan as she always prefers to come here because at hers, The Neat Freak's always checking we're keeping everything tidy. Sorrel is relieved to get out of the house as she's finding it exhausting to be around Ray and Yolanda knowing about the incident with the Beast Car. Apparently Ray keeps coming up to Sorrel and whispering, 'You won't say anything, will you?' and it's getting on her nerves.

Mum got The Impostor to blow up a couple of airbeds, not realizing that the sleepover is all part of my cunning Beat The Impostor plan. This involves one of us staying awake at all times, so that if Mum and The Impostor come in late and try to make it up the stairs, one of us will be waiting, ready to ambush them. I'll also make sure that someone goes downstairs at regular intervals to get a glass of water. That should put them off any sofa-grappling.

I'm also going to ask the girls to do something which sounds really pervy, but isn't, which is to have a look at my boobs and let me know if they think they *are* different sizes, or whether I'm just becoming para over the mono-boob issue. I thought about getting them to take a series of pictures with my digi camera as a record, but then I decided I'd be forever freaking out that the shots would get into the wrong hands, say, if I died and Jack inherited my camera, and instead of being viewed as the medical record of a monoboobite, they'd be seen as an amateur porno-fest by a group of teenage girls.

'School OK?' The Impostor throws a question out into the icy atmosphere.

'Yep,' I bat back.

There's a pause before he tries again.

'I know it's years away, but any idea what you might like to do when you leave school?'

'Nope.'

Electra Brown versus The Impostor, and Miss Brown is winning hands down!

'Do you like rock music?'

'Yep.' The saddo has probably been sniffing around my room looking for topics he can use as conversation. I'll need to tape some thread traps across the doorframe to catch him out.

The Impostor doesn't say anything for a bit, but I can hear him shuffle around on the hard chair. Perhaps as he hasn't got kids he doesn't realize what the sullen monosyllabic combo is supposed to signify. Perhaps he thinks this is how *all* teenagers act.

Just when I think he's decided to give up getting

284

me to speak he says, 'Why do you never smile when I'm around?'

I'm searching for a single-syllable answer, when he carries on. 'I saw you smile when we first met so I know that you *can* smile. I remember thinking what a great name Electra was for you as you were so bright and sparky, but now you hardly speak. I get the impression you don't like me very much.'

Damn! I can't instantly think of a one-word cutting retort. I could shrug but that's not really allowed in the monosyllabic game. You've got to say *something*. I think I've struck lucky when I think of, 'So?'

'So, why not?'

I'm stuck. If I say 'Dunno' that's two syllables and the game will be over. So if I *have* to break the game, I might as well do it in spectacular style. I still don't have to smile.

I fling down my mag, haul myself up off the sofa, stand with my arms crossed across my uneven and pathetic chest and say accusingly, 'I think you just drive around the place fixing cars and picking up vulnerable women and then wheedle your way into their lives and their beds by making yourself useful around the house. Jack might be impressed by your big truck and flashing yellow lights, and Mum might be flattered that you know what to do with her spark plugs, but that doesn't wash with me, right?'

'Ouch!' The Impostor pretends he's been stabbed in the stomach. 'Don't spare me, will you?'

'Well, *you* asked.'

'I guess I did.'

For a man whose personality I've just trashed, he seems surprisingly calm.

'Ellie and I are just friends,' he says. 'That's all.'

'Yeah, right. But I bet you want more.'

I fully expect him to give me some speech about how he hasn't even thought of my mum in that way and how he's offended I could say such a thing, but he just says, 'I'm not going to lie to you. The moment I saw your mum sitting on that bank on the dual carriageway I felt something special.'

'I *bet* you did,' I sneer, 'especially when you saw her dig that receipt out of her boobs!'

The Impostor roars with laughter. 'Well, I couldn't miss that, could I? But it's too soon for her, *much* too soon. My parents divorced and I'm divorced so I know what it's like.'

'Mum and Dad are just separated, *not* divorced.' I'm keen to let The Impostor know that they're still married. 'Anyway, you said you get on with your ex. It's not the same thing at all.'

The Impostor smiles. 'Well, we get on now, but we didn't. It was pretty poisonous at the time.'

'Serves you right for having an affair!' I snap.

'Me? An affair?' The Impostor raises his eyebrows. 'Oh, don't assume it's always the men! I was in the army and whilst I was away fighting for Queen and country, Debs, my ex, was having an affair with her fitness instructor!'

I feel a slug-head. 'Sorry,' I mutter.

The Impostor waves my apology away. 'Look, it's fine. I can see how it happened, I was away a lot and . . .' His voice trails off. 'It was a shame because she looked really fit just before she left me, what with all that extra tuition!'

He laughs at the memory and I *so* want to smile with him but I'm not going to. I've broken the monosyllabic vow, but the vow of sullency *must* remain intact.

'When did your parents divorce?' I ask, hoping that my face is looking particularly stony.

'When I was about fifteen. My dad married again a few years later and I lived with Mum. I was a right plonker to all her boyfriends so in the end she just gave up dating. She's been on her own for the last twenty-five years.'

I hear Mum flushing the loo upstairs. I don't want her on her own for twenty-five years, but I don't want The Impostor around either. Mum and Dad will never get back together if he is, and the fact that Dad seems unhappy with The Bitch Troll has given me hope of a parental reconciliation.

'I can only mend cars, not broken hearts,' The Impostor says.

'Cheesy!' I say, but by now, I'm desperate to at least smirk. I'm trying my best to give The Impostor a hard time but he's not having any of it.

Mum comes down the stairs. She looks tired and a little drained, but lovely. With her being just Mum, I sometimes forget how young she is, much younger than either Bella or Yolanda. The dress she's wearing is a bit big on account of her weight loss, though the Mighty Mammaries seem not to have been affected by the stress diet and are still out front and proud.

'Ellie, you look fantastic!' says Phil. His eyes are shining, *and* he's looking at her face, not the Mighty Mammaries.

Mum blushes and laughs off the compliment with a breezy, 'Oh, this old thing?' but she seems to be shining too.

I should feel pleased that Mum seems happy for the first time in months, but I feel pissed off and left out. It's come to something when your mum is going out on a Saturday night date whilst you're stuck in waiting for your friends to come round to act as referees in the great *Am I a monoboobite?* debate.

'Will you be OK, Electra?' Mum's fiddling around in her bag.

I flop back down on the sofa, pick up my mag and say tartly, 'Oh, why worry about me. No one else does.'

'Well, I've got my mobile if you need me.'

'Whatever.'

'You've got the number for the restaurant?'

'Yeah.'

'What time are the girls coming round?'

'Soon.'

'Are you *sure* you're OK?'

Mum's last question provides me with a perfect test. I clutch my stomach and say in a whiney voice, 'Well, actually, I feel pretty ropey, but you two just go off and have a good time. I can ring for an ambulance if the pains get worse.'

There's a tense silence in the kitchen, and I peer round the edge of *Teen Vogue*. The Impostor is looking at his watch and Mum is looking at me. She knows I'm playing up, but I can tell she's on the verge of cancelling the evening. Her eyes, which moments ago were sparkling at the excitement of a rare evening out, are now hooded with anxiety.

I feel a prime bitch. There's nothing wrong with me except a severe bout of jealousy and teenage sullenness.

'Phil, look, maybe this wasn't such a good idea.' Mum's voice sounds thick with disappointment.

'No, you go,' I say. 'I'll be fine.'

I'm *totally* shocked when they instantly take me at my word. I'd expected at least one more round of 'No, we won't go.' 'Yes, go.' I hear them going up the stairs. I know that Mum will be worrying all evening about me, even though she knows I'm not really ill. It'll put her off her garlic bread and prawn linguine, and after the cabbage-soup-and-divorce diet she really deserves a good dose of carbs.

I jump off the sofa and rush upstairs, just as they're walking out through the front door.

'Wait!' I shriek.

They turn and I can tell Mum is thinking, *Oh no, what now?*

The Impostor still looks calm and smiley, though if I were him I'd want to strangle me.

I look him straight in the eyes. 'I've just got one thing to say to you. Do you like aubergines?'

Phil Harris doesn't do the whole fruit-machine face that Candy Baxter did. He doesn't look confused, wondering what the right answer to the question is. He's not trying to impress me. He just says, 'Those evil purple blobs make me want to gag. Why?'

'Oh, no reason,' I say, smiling. 'Have a lovely time, but bring Mum back sober!'

Chapter Thirty

Some things sound so perfect together, it would be weird to think of them paired with anything else.

Fish and chips.

Bread and butter.

Knife and fork.

Peaches and cream.

Me and Jags.

OK, so maybe not the last one, but with the others, if you change one of the pair to, say, fish and cabbage, or peaches and ketchup it sounds all wrong. Probably tastes rank too, though I imagine if you ate fish and cabbage often enough you'd get used to it.

I thought my parents suited each other perfectly however you described them: Mum and Dad, Ellie and Rob, Mr and Mrs Brown, but like fish and chips rather fish and cabbage, was that just because it was all I knew?

And what happens now there's not Mum *and* Dad, but Mum, and Dad?

If Mum does start going out with Phil it will be Ellie and Phil, Mrs Brown and Mr Harris or Mum and Phil. To me, all of these combinations sound as wrong as fish and cabbage, but not as disgusting as Rob and Candy, which will *never* sound right.

And what if Candy and Dad get married? She'll then become Mrs Brown, so there'll be two Mrs Browns, unless Mum goes back to her maiden name of Stafford.

It's all so confusing, but in my mind there'll only ever be one Mr and Mrs Brown, and that's *my* mum and dad.

A few months ago I didn't think my names went together: Electra, the pervy porn star first name and Brown, the bog-standard surname. But you know what, even if I do get married (to Jags, obviously!) I think I'll keep my name rather than change it to my husband's. Electra Garcia sounds great, but Electra Brown sounds right.

I still don't look like an Electra. I haven't morphed into an exotic moussaka-munching temptress. As for its meaning, I'm still not bright, but my grades in geography have shot up thanks to Buff Butler. But I *feel* like Electra Brown. My name's a bit of Mum and a bit of Dad and a reminder of the good times when they first got married.

No one can take the past away, whether there's a Candy or a Phil or anyone else hanging around. So even though they're not together any more, actually, I don't need to worry. To me and Jack they'll always be Mum and Dad *whatever* their surnames or whoever they're with.

Whoever said, 'Like father like son,' and 'Like mother like daughter,' wasn't totally correct. It's not as simple as that. You inherit the good bits and the bad bits from both sides.

What they should have said was, 'Like father *and* mother.'

About the Author

Helen Bailey was born and brought up in Ponteland, Newcastle-upon-Tyne. Barely into her teens, Helen invested her pocket money in a copy of *The Writers' and Artists' Yearbook* and spent the next few years sending short stories and poems to anyone she could think of. Much to her surprise, she sometimes found herself in print. After a degree in science, Helen worked in the media and now runs a successful London-based character licensing agency handling internationally renowned properties such as Snoopy, Dirty Dancing, Dilbert and Felicity Wishes. With her dachshund, Rufus, and her husband, John, she divides her time between Highgate, north London and the north-east. She is the author of a number of short stories, young novels and picture books.

www.helenbaileybooks.com

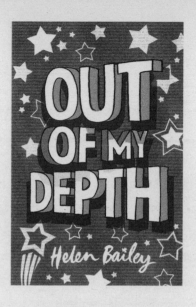

I am *totally*
out of my depth.

**Everyone's giving me the third degree!
Freak Boy's dad wants to know whether he's being bullied.
Sorrel's interrogating me about Lucy's stroppy moods.**

**Even Dad is cross-examining me about Mum's
love-life, over garlic bread and pepperoni pizza.**

**And all I can think is, *How far can you get a piece
of melted cheese to stretch without it breaking?***

I can be **very shallow.**

**These are the real-life,
messed-up rants of me,
Electra Brown. Welcome to my crazy world.**

destiny is before you. A quite different road is before me. The story goes on, the tale never ends. As far as the Signs are concerned . . . There is one you don't know. It's called the Somne. Look at my hand.'

She looked.

'An illusion,' she heard from somewhere, far away. 'Everything is an illusion.'

'I say, wench! Don't sleep or you'll be robbed!'

She jerked her head up. Rubbed her eyes. And sprang up from the ground.

'Did I fall asleep? Was I sleeping?'

'I should say!' laughed a stout woman from the driver's box of a wagon. 'Like a log! Like a baby! I hailed you twice – nothing. I was about to get off the cart . . . Are you alone? Why are you looking around? Are you looking for someone?'

'For a man . . . with white hair . . . He was here . . . Or maybe . . . I don't know myself.'

'I didn't see anyone,' replied the woman. The little heads of two children peered out from under the tarpaulin behind her.

'I heed that you're travelling,' said the woman, indicating with her eyes Nimue's bundle and stick. 'I'm driving to Dorian. I'll take you if you wish. If you're going that way.'

'Thanks,' said Nimue, clambering up onto the box. 'Thanks a hundredfold.'

'That's the way!' The woman cracked the reins. 'Then we'll go! It's more comfortable to ride than hoof it, isn't? Oh, you must have been fair beat to doze off and lay down right beside the road. You were sleeping, I tell you—'

'—like a log,' Nimue sighed. 'I know. I was weary and fell asleep. And what's more, I had—'

'Yes? What did you have?'

She looked back. Behind her was the black forest. Before her was the road, running between an avenue of willows. A road towards destiny.

The story goes on, she thought. *The story never ends.*

'—a very strange dream.'

359